ALIEN REVEALED

The Confederation Treaty Book 1

LILLY CAIN

Alien Revealed

Crash landing on the Earth military base I'd been watching was never part of the plan. But it happened. And what I learned there will change the Confederacy forever. Because I've found what we've been looking for - a species who can join us in m'ittar - mind contact that makes love a possibility. I am Agent Alinna Gaerrii and my family's standing will either fall or soar with what happens next.

My dreams have been invaded. Not that I'm complaining, but they've never been so real. They always feature the woman I rescued from the wreckage of a plane crash near my base. A woman who will make or break my career as the leader of a special force headed to space - the psychologist sent to evaluate my team. Or is she? Major David Brown reporting for duty and definitely suspicious.

Save each other, save their people. It's time for humans to join the Confederacy. If they can.

Part One of the Confederacy Treaty

Alien Revealed
The Confederation Treaty Series Book 1

Lilly Cain

ISBN 978-1-989138-01-4

Cover design by Candace Phillips Gilmer
Flirtation Designs

Discover other titles by Lilly Cain www.lillycain.com

To friends and readers old and new.

Chapter 1

"I repeat this is Agent Alinna Gaerrii, Unit Nine. *Tel sho ahoi.* I am in a crash situation." Alinna called out the codes in Inarrii and in Standard English in case she was picked up by the Human military base she was about to crash land on. They shouldn't be aware of her presence, but under the circumstances, if they *did* hear her, at least they would likely assume they were getting a garbled report of the now burning Human airjet on the ground. Thankfully, the local dialect had been ingrained in her consciousness after six months of intense monitoring and translation of their communications.

The altimeter pulsed; the glowing lines flashing an alarming blue. Manual control levers slid up and out into the limited space where she could reach them and she grabbed the double-barred shaft as the automatic flight comp in the little pod signaled its inability to recover the necessary height for ultrasonic flight.

She was going down. Her small observation pod hurtled toward the ground at an ever-increasing rate. Caught in the downdraft of an out-of-control Human airjet, her tiny spy craft seemed as doomed as the vehicle that had crashed to the ground in front of her moments ago. Shuddering sensations raced up Alinna's arms and along her scalp. Her *l'inar* nerve lines forced her skin up into narrow bands and ridges along her neck and hairline in an instinctual reaction as her concern turned quickly into fear.

Why had she let herself get so close?

Her pod was not meant for this kind of action. A tiny craft rigged to avoid Human detection, it was only meant for short-term surveillance. There was barely enough room on board for her long body to lie flat against the monitoring equipment. Her mission was simple—park her ship on the Humans' home planet moon and use her pod to move in close enough to observe Human behavior for a few days at a time—to watch, but not interact. *But I am going to interact; they're going to have to peel my Inarrü skin right off their shiny new Starforce facilities.* Moisture beaded on her forehead as Alinna fought to regain control of the pod, wrenching the manual controls up and back until they pressed against her chest.

Warning lights flashed. Her altitude was dropping erratically. "No shit," she said aloud. Six months of listening to the Humans' fondness for verbal vulgarity was rubbing off. She'd been observing a heated argument on the ground with some amusement when the Human airjet took her by surprise, veering suddenly off its scheduled course and into the airspace above the woods surrounding the new military base. Swerving right into her path, its engine had disrupted the ultrasonic pulse waves that kept her pod safely aloft. In seconds, the airjet had crashed to the ground and erupted in flames while she watched in horror, unable to do anything other than struggle for control over her own vehicle. The airjet had broken into three jagged, fiery pieces; there was little likelihood anyone survived.

The automated emergency beacon started to flash as Alinna gave up trying to recover and instead braced for impact. The tips of treetops snapped hard against the outer shell of her pod, twisting the small craft into a spin. Alinna held on, her heart pounding. Her curving *L'inar* nerve lines were tight and burning in alarm over most of her body, from her scalp to her toes, leaving only her face, palms, and the flat of her feet free of the sensation. The fall took forever, the last of the ultrasonic waves battering the tiny ship against the tall spikes of Earth vegetation. Then, with one final nauseating drop, the craft hit the ground.

Alinna lay stunned inside her pod. For a moment, she ignored the screaming monitors around her. *I'm alive.* Then the sharp scent of ozone caught her attention. The warnings flashing and beeping around her suddenly had meaning again. She scrambled to unfasten her harness and wiggle her way to the escape hatch at the front of the craft. She snarled in frustration when the latch release refused to operate. Time to get out—now. Urgency flooded endorphins through her body, lending her a full measure of Inarrii strength.

Alinna slammed the hatch completely open as a shudder rippled through the ship. She could smell smoke. Security measures dictated she would need to hide the craft while on alien soil, but at this rate she wondered if there would be anything left to hide. She dragged her body through the narrow hatch, grabbing her emergency pouch on the way out. *This was so much easier in the escape simulations.* Disembarking was simple when she was in the weightless docking bay of her larger vessel—still secreted and now completely inaccessible in a crater on the dark side of the Earth's moon.

Alinna scrambled to her knees on the thick carpet of vegetation outside her ship. She staggered as she rose to her feet and moved away from the small craft. Taking refuge under the sagging bows of a huge tree, she stared at her ruined vessel. The Human airjet had destroyed the ultrasonic wave pattern keeping her aloft, but she could have recovered if she'd been a little higher. But in the business of surveillance, being close to the subject was a necessary risk. It was the landing that had wrecked it, the landing and being bounced and smashed against the trees on the way down. The branches of the massive vegiforms around her had slowed her enough to save her life, but the pod was done.

A soft breeze brought again the acrid stench of smoke. The Human airjet was burning nearby and would surely have military attention at any moment. She needed to get rid of the pod and hide. She tapped the skin at the base of her left ear, initiating her internal command unit. Without much hope, she requested total silent mode for the pod. Before her, a shimmer of light flickered over the craft as it attempted to initiate the power field to make it once again invisible to the naked eye or casual scan. She grimaced. Nothing happened. *Not surprising, after the beating the vessel took on the way down.*

"*Kahemnit dal,*" she whispered. "Shit." The Human curse sounded more satisfying, and certainly more graphic. An errant breeze flipped a lock of her shoulder-length brown hair into her eyes. She blew it away from her face with a huff of annoyance. She had no choice. She had to destroy the ship. "*Tel sho ahoi, sho amnetii.*" Alinna used her internal command unit to access her damaged craft's communication system to signal her people, hidden far away on the secret Jupiter Moon Base. With luck, they would hear her, although she might never know what they thought of her decision. They could not respond to her; any incoming communication held a much higher risk of detection than her brief message out.

"I am initiating *sho amnetii gohan yi*." She began the short self-destruct sequence, pursing her lips and hoping it would work. If the ship was too damaged for this last function, she would have to find some way to destroy or hide it herself. That might not be possible, having crash landed on the outskirts of the heavily guarded Human Starforce base she'd been sent to survey. She scanned the woods. She was going to need a more secure hiding spot, and soon. If she was discovered by the Humans, the mission would be a total loss, spelling disaster for her career, a huge loss of honor for her family, and serious trouble for the eventual first contact between the Inarrii and Humans.

Alinna stepped away from the shelter of the tree and shivered as a cool breeze brushed against her legs. She felt wet. Confused, she looked down at her legs and was shocked at the sight of a long piece of metal piercing the heavy material of her blue flight suit. Blood ran freely from the injury in her calf. As if the sight of the wound suddenly made it a reality, pain swept through her body. She staggered. A soft moan slipped from her lips as she realized how badly she was injured. Pain blossomed in her head as well, making her wonder if she'd also suffered a concussion during her abrupt drop to Earth. Before her, waves of heat rose from her tiny spy pod. At least the self-destruct appeared to be working.

She staggered away from the craft, trying to get out of range as it used its own components to create a chemical reaction to reduce the vehicle to a tiny puddle of melted plastics. After perhaps a half dozen steps, she fell to her knees. Something had to be done with the material in her leg—that too needed to be destroyed. Silently she thanked her ancestors that it hadn't ripped into any of her L'inar, an injury that would have spelled doom and death more surely than surely than anything else. A hard yank and she ripped it from her body and threw it toward the reacting pod. Then she turned and vomited from the pain, shadows dancing across her vision.

On her hands and knees she crawled farther from the craft. If she could make it to the trees she might stay hidden. Only a few seconds later her vision receded to a murky grey. She flicked on her internal comp's smart mode, since the realization she was about to be unconscious was inescapable. Maybe it could think of a way out of this. At the very least it would continue to gather information and pass on her fate if her people ever came close enough to download the intel. Maybe that would be enough to restore her honor after her failure to stay hidden reached the council.

Out of the corner of her eye, bright lights flashed. Search lights, likely, from the lumbering flight of another Human aircraft headed straight toward the crash site, and her. Then everything faded to darkness, the scent of melting plastic strong against the fresh scent of broken vegetation.

MAJOR DAVID BROWN cursed softly under his breath. What he didn't need right now was another delay. Not for any reason. He had two weeks until the newest Starforce mission team would be assembled, and he planned to be on it as team leader, and his crew with him. Instead, he was sitting with his Starforce pilots in the back of a heli-jet on their way to a crash site. He grabbed the handle above his seat as turbulence interrupted his thoughts—high winds taking their toll on the impromptu rescue team's combination helicopter-jet. He shook his head. Their orders were to find and investigate a military airjet that had sent out distress signals and apparently gone down in the acres of woods near the base.

The team assembly would have to wait. Lives were at stake, and the base was undermanned. Recent transfers and the opening of a newer, larger base at the other end of the state had moved out so much staff that he and the other pilots currently residing on the base had been forced to take up security positions for this unforeseen disaster. And security, an absolute must on the top secret base, had number one priority. At least that was what command thought. Personally, saving a life would be his priority, although in a crash situation there were probably no survivors.

Still, security was undoubtedly at risk if someone had shot down a military airjet right on their border.

David frowned. The team assignment would wait anyway. According to the latest scuttle, all possible candidates for the new mission had to be reevaluated by yet another team of psychtechs. He, in particular, was about to be closely scrutinized, tested yet again for fitness of duty for long-term space travel and command. The why of the countless tests escaped him, but no one was offering explanations at this point.

"Base to unit seven-oh-seven." The message came across an open channel.

David tapped the compad on the side of his helmet. "Unit seven-oh-seven here."

"We have communication for Major Brown."

"This is Major Brown," David replied steadily despite the sensation of several pairs of eyes now focused on him.

"Major Brown, we have received satellite confirmation that airjet four-two-niner is down and burning on sector Alpha-Charlie-seven-niner."

"Understood."

"We have also been informed the roster was empty except for the two male air force pilots and one Dr. Janet MacPherson, a civilian assigned to your team."

David blinked. *Damn.* Muttering began in the back of the heli-jet. News traveled faster in the ranks than laser fire. There was no sense trying to keep rumors silent—pressure to do so only made the rumors fly faster. "Copy. Unit seven-oh-seven out."

So the psychtech had been on board. He mulled that fact over, along with the reality that few people ever survived an airjet crash. While he regretted the loss of any life, a thought lurked like a shadow in his mind. *If she's dead, they'll postpone the mission…or more likely, they'll pull an officer in from another team who's already been checked out to replace me and get the job done with no more delays.* Either thought left him cold.

"ETA two minutes, Major Brown."

David could already feel the deceleration of the heli-jet. Small and maneuverable, the vehicle covered the huge base in minutes and could land in a space smaller than his quarters. He held up a closed fist to his team, five of the best pilots in Starforce. They wouldn't normally risk the skills these men and women had in a rescue mission, even in the understaffed status of the base, but the base was undermanned on purpose. As well as the recent opening of a new, larger base taking some of the staff, operations here were intended to be top secret, and the fewer people involved, the better. Besides, his pilots were getting antsy waiting for the mission to be assigned. A little action was a good thing.

"Lee, Yancy, you two are on left flank. Olens, Huff, and Branscombe, you go to the right. Look for the airjet comp unit."

"What about survivors?" First Lieutenant Angie Lee called out.

"There aren't likely to be any, but see if you can ID any bodies. Three in total."

"Savvy," she agreed.

The heli-jet touched down, its landing a gentle bump. The team filed out while David waited near the pilot. He slapped a hand to the pilot's shoulder. "Round us up in ten minutes."

"Understood, Major."

David stepped out of the heli-jet and into hell. The light breeze blew smoke directly into his face. The airjet lay broken into three pieces like a discarded toy before him, and the tail end was burning. He clamped his lips shut against the noxious smell of charred plasmetal alloy. *There's no way anyone lived through this.* The grim thought barely passed through his mind when he heard shouts from his team on the left flank of the crash site. He jogged steadily toward the group, his eyes quickly focusing on his team and on Lieutenant Lee's kneeling position over what had to be a crash victim.

David leapt over a few tree roots and neatly avoided thick pine branches broken off by the fallen airjet. The scene struck him as surreal. In a world with little vegetation left, they were all invaders in this pocket of wilderness. At a better time, he might have enjoyed the scent of pine, the cool of the shaded woods. In moments, he too stood over the body of a woman, her features slack and the left leg of her blue jumper ripped and coated in blood.

He shook his head and grimaced. "Dr. MacPherson."

"She's alive, Major!" Lieutenant Lee was already hauling out her emergency medkit.

"What?" Adrenalin flooded his body. He'd been ready to accept the psychtech's loss, but the situation had changed. She needed his help, now. "Lieutenant Yancy, get that autolift from the heli-jet." He tapped his helmet's compad. "Unit seven-oh-seven to base—we have a survivor and need immediate medical attention."

David switched his attention back to the injured woman. Her light brown hair spread around her on the ground. Lee was working fast, applying a compress to the woman's leg until they could get her to the medtechs. The psychtech moaned, tilting her head to one side and exposing a series of intricate tattoos running from her scalp down the length of her neck, their color varying from rust to a dark brown. David frowned. They looked like the tattoos favorable a few years ago for underground groups wanting to align with their cultural backgrounds, usually tree-hugging low techs. *What kind of military psychologist wears cultural tats?*

He tapped his compad. "Branscombe, how's it look over there?"

"No sign of comp or vics."

A soft moan brought David's attention back to the injured doctor. Her eyelids fluttered, revealing unusually bright green eyes. *"Gohan yi…"* she murmured before passing out again. Lieutenant Lee looked up at him, a question in her eyes, but David shrugged. Hard to say what the woman was trying to get out at this point. Or even what language she was speaking. But she'd live, and they could question her later.

"Major," Captain Sue Branscombe's voice called over the compad and through the air simultaneously. Her team had worked its way to the other side of the wreck and now stood several yards away, near another set of giant pine trees. She waved to him, indicating he should come to their location, and he signaled that he would in a moment. Lieutenant Tom Yancy arrived with the autolift, walking beside it as it glided above the air on an ultrasonic wave. Its low, vibrating hum played counterpoint to the staccato sound of the burning airjet. David caught one edge of the lift and steadied it as Yancy signaled it for descent, then helped him slide the doctor's unconscious body onto the flat surface.

"Get her back to the medlab and stay with her. Have the heli-jet come back for us." David kept his eyes on the woman's face. She remained unconscious, her smooth skin pale and unlined. Without the bright green of her eyes and her unusual tattoos, she could be anyone, or no one, but this was the woman who would make or break his space career.

Lieutenant Yancy grunted an agreement and began to walk the autolift back to the heli-jet, carefully stepping over the uneven ground as he guided the unit. David watched them for a moment and then strode toward his second team. He glanced down at the ground and caught sight of the wet reflection of light on tiny droplets of blood spattered over fallen leaves. Dr. MacPherson must have come from this direction, as well. He tracked the drops as he walked, noting the amount of blood seemed to be greater as he reached his pilots.

"Major, check this out," Branscombe called to him, her strident voice ringing with impatience.

"Is it the airjet comp?"

"Nope. We don't know what the hell it is."

On that cryptic note, David moved a little faster. The blood trail also expanded, as if Dr. MacPherson had paused for a few minutes here. David stepped to one side of his pilots, careful not to disturb a small pool of blood. Branscombe and the other two pilots stood staring at the ground. The scent of pine hung heavy in the air. David stepped over another broken pine branch and glanced up at the tree canopy as a small shower of pine needles rained down on him. At least a dozen other branches were twisted and broken in the trees above.

The smell of burning plastics overrode the aroma of pine once again, and David flicked his gaze back to the ground near his team's feet. A puddle of melted plastic lay in a long oval shape, some of it clearly being absorbed into the soft bed of needles and soil. He'd never seen anything like it.

"Is it part of the airjet?" David squatted down to get a little closer to the material.

"If it is, I can't imagine what it was or why it would just…melt like this."

David frowned. He knew the personnel on board the airjet, but what about cargo? Had the aircraft contained something dangerous? News on the upcoming mission was tight, and there'd been little explanation as to why a group of interplanetary settlers needed a full flight team for defense. Perhaps what lay on the ground was a hint of why the mission was so secretive. "Any of you got a sample kit on you?"

"I do." Second Lieutenant Sven Olens, the biggest bruiser David had ever met, pulled a small kit from his backpack.

"Take a sample of whatever the hell this is, and of some of the soil around here too. Branscombe, you got record mode?"

"On for the duration, Major."

She would have filmed their search and the discovery here. "Any sign of the airjet comp or the rest of the crew?"

"No, but a lot of the wreckage is too burned to ID much of anything."

"The flames are nearly out. When they called us in, they didn't expect a long burn or call for firefighters. No one expected to find much of anything. I think the comp is still on board, and further survivors highly unlikely. Do we all agree?"

"Agreed." Branscombe spoke for the rest. At thirty-nine, she was the oldest pilot applying for the Starforce defense mission, but she was also the best, and his second in command.

"Good. File out and search again for the comp or bodies, but after that I think we'll hand the rest of the search over to the clean-up crew. Nothing we can do here now."

"I can't believe that anyone lived through it." Lieutenant George Huff shook his head. "It's amazing, savvy?"

"Damn right." David looked down at the puddle of Dr. MacPherson's blood. *She'd survived. And she saw what happened here. Perhaps the psychtech knows more about this mission than I do.*

Chapter 2

Alinna counted four. Four Humans in her immediate vicinity who would have to have their memories altered if her mission was to continue. She grimaced, keeping her eyes closed. She could sense their emotional signatures as easily as looking at them. Let them think she was still unconscious. Pain radiated up her leg, making it clear that the Human medtechs could benefit greatly from Inarrii medical technology. But that wasn't her major problem. No, she could well imagine how this was going to go when she somehow managed to report in to her commanding officer. To have to call an Examiner down to alter memories...she'd never be put on an active mission again.

Two medtechs stood in the corridor outside her room, performing their various duties. An administrator sat at a desk farther down the hall. Alinna could sense their emotions; excitement over her being alive and relief over the at least temporary cessation of boredom. Her Inarrii senses might be less powerful than some—she could only sense emotion and not specific thoughts without physical contact—but for her work, emotions were more reliable than direct thoughts and far more difficult to hide. Everyone in the building was hurried, but calm in the certainty of their work. No alarm radiated; no suspicion or dread over finding an alien in their woods projected into the ether. This was a surprise. Obviously the results from her blood analysis couldn't be back yet or they would understand she was far from Human. Her attention focused on the one mind that didn't seem to belong. He was approaching her room. *No, he's in my room.*

His emotions were clouded, but his focus was on her. She couldn't wait any longer. She opened her eyes to look at the man who now stood only an arm's length away. Immediately sexual interest flared along her sensitive *L'inar* nerve lines, telegraphing pleasure throughout her body. Tall and muscular, he could have been Inarrii if not for the lack of *L'inar* and for his deep blue eyes. Shortly cropped dark hair, styled in tiny spikes no Inarrii male would sport, and freckled skin completed the differences, but his commanding presence and clear concern over her well-being attracted her in much the same way an Inarrii male displaying the same level of attention would. He cared, and deep in his emotional psyche, behind the concern and other factors, she could sense a returned attraction.

Get it under control, she chastised herself. *This Human will have to have his memories altered, as well. No one can know yet of our presence here.* Of course, if the Humans turned out to be a people the Inarrii complement felt would work with the Intergalactic Confederacy, the people here on the Starforce base would be some of the first to be contacted. *I'd like to be the one to contact him,* she admitted to herself.

Some of her interest must have shown in her eyes. The man glanced away, slight color rising along his high cheekbones. From her studies of Human culture, she understood that sexual interest was carefully controlled in the military, but his flushing skin gave him away.

"Dr. MacPherson, I'm glad to see you are recovering quickly."

Alinna blinked. Her mind raced. They had no idea who she really was but had assigned an identity to her, one she had no clue about. *I should have checked the god's blessed comp smart mode the minute I woke.* She cleared her throat, intensely grateful for all those hours translating Standard English. "Yes…what happened? Where am I?"

"We're hoping you can tell us. I'm Major David Brown. You were assigned to asses my team for duty and were on your way to Starforce Base One when your airjet went down. We haven't yet ascertained the cause of the crash, but you are the only survivor."

She knew him. The realization shook her. She'd listened to that rich, deep voice, seen his muscular body in action from afar as she'd spied on the base. The familiarity made it worse somehow. She'd enjoyed watching him. With his eyes focused on her, Alinna fought the urge to shift away. Inarrii didn't lie well. Normally they didn't lie at all. This was one of the reasons that despite looking very similar to Humans, Inarrii were restricted to peripheral observation, no contact. Later, if things progressed to the point where a treaty would be negotiated, their similar features would be an asset, as would their reputation for honesty. Now she had to lie, or at least avoid the truth.

She sat up in the bed, figuring at this point that action was less revealing than words. As she swung her legs out from under the covers, she discovered she'd been dressed in a loose-fitting gown. Her *L'inar* were mostly covered, but she felt the major's interest sharpen as a few of the stray markings on the inside of her elbows and lower arms were exposed by her movements. She fought to keep any reaction under control. He couldn't know his interest was causing tingles of desire to run the curving lengths of her *L'inar*. The sensitive nerves curled and wrapped around her body, the swirls of color on her skin betraying only a hint of how the sensors interacted within her. In males, the *L'inar* rose into tight ridges when they were sexually excited. For females that only happened in fear. In a sexual reaction they heated her, spreading pleasure from her skin to all the most sensitive areas of her body.

Alinna suppressed a moan. It had been a long time since she'd relieved her stress with an Inarrii male. Sex helped them control their emotions—an important ability in a race with telepathic and empathic abilities. Her anxiety at the moment, and the heady male attention from Major Brown, had her weak in the knees. She needed a clear head and struggled for control. She'd just been presented with an opportunity, if she dared to use it. The Humans thought she was someone expected to work on the base. They didn't realize she was a spy, or that she wasn't even Human. She could, for a short time at least, blend in and learn far more than she or her superiors had ever expected to discover about the Humans. Meeting with them, working with them, would answer unequivocally the question as to whether they could work together within the Confederacy.

But at the moment, it was too much. Between the stress, her injury and the major's attention, her senses were on overload. She stood, and the room spun around her. When the major caught her by the elbow as she began to sway, he inadvertently touched a curl of her *L'inar*. She gasped as pleasure rocketed from the casual touch straight to her core. She clutched his arm, frantically trying to gain control.

"Be careful. You've been through a lot, Doctor." Major Brown's deep voice increased the tension in her body.

Alinna inhaled, immediately realizing her mistake as she took in the spicy cologne that mixed with his own heady male scent. "Ummm…" Her words stalled. He was truly as tall as any Inarrii male; she had to tilt her head slightly to meet his deep blue eyes. For a moment, she swam in their depths. Neither moved.

———————

DAVID SET the doctor back on her bed where she belonged. The fact that he would rather have kept her in his arms was not lost to him. Awake now, with those emerald eyes looking so deeply into his, he had the sudden revelation that the next two weeks might be far harder than he had suspected. Not only would he have to survive yet another round of psychological testing, but along with the stress of awaiting the upcoming mission, he would have to keep every moment of his time with the doctor under control. He would love to taste those luscious lips, test the softness of her skin against his. But she was the one calling the shots in his life. One slip, one moment of questionable behavior around her, and his career would be at an end.

Besides, a question remained at the back of his mind.

"Do you remember anything about the time of the crash? Or immediately after?"

She looked away from him and caught the edge of her medical gown between her fingers, running them along its hem.

He narrowed his eyes at her. She did know something. He could see it in her demeanor, the way she held her shoulders. That in itself was strange. A psychtech at the level she must be to have received a posting on the Starforce base should be well aware of body language, both how to read it and control it. Perhaps the shock of the crash had her off balance.

"Not really. I remember hearing the pilot call out, and the emergency signal. Then nothing until I awoke here, met you."

There was something in her inflection when she said "you." "You recognize my name?"

"Yes."

"You've been assigned to my team as psychtech to provide the final psych tests and give the green light on the mission."

"Green light...right."

Something just wasn't right. She hesitated before she made each statement. Granted, she could still be somewhat disoriented from the crash and from the pain medication. "You *are* Dr. Janet MacPherson, correct?"

She sat up straighter, looked him dead in the eye. "Yes, but call me Alinna—all my friends do." She smiled and the expression blew him away. With her grin came a sexiness that even her fabulous eyes hadn't hinted at. That smile matched her wild tattoos in a way that made parts of him sit up and take notice.

"I'm sorry, Major Brown." A young female medtech bustled into the room and touched his elbow. "You'll have to go. Dr. MacPherson needs her rest. She'll be released tomorrow, and then she's all yours. But for tonight, she's mine."

David clenched his teeth against the comment that so desperately wanted to escape his lips. He wanted the doctor to be his, all right, just not in the manner the medtech assumed. *Probably not how the doctor assumes either,* he thought with disgust. He had to regain his control. She'd hardly be putting a stamp of approval on a leader who wanted to claim his doctor in a very personal way when she was still recovering from a crash. Or at all, for that matter.

"I'll see you then in the morning, Dr. MacPherson."

"Alinna, please."

He smiled wryly at her. She would know that sort of familiarity was frowned upon, and he'd served for long enough that a psychtech trying to be familiar with him sent off warning bells. Not to mention that the nickname seemed fairly odd. Instead he tried for a foray of his own. "Doctor, I'll be here at oh-nine-hundred to escort you through the proper channels for outfitting and room assignment, since your things—along with all of the airjet's freight—were destroyed." He watched her face carefully, but there was no reaction about the lost cargo. She either knew it was destroyed already or really didn't care. Perhaps the melted plastic had been just that—debris.

She nodded and he turned to leave. At the doorway, he turned back.

"Have a good night, Dr. MacPherson. But if you think of anything about the crash that we should know here, I hope you will call me. Your interlink is active on the nightstand." He motioned to the small screen on a table near her elbow. "Call me if you can remember anything at all, Doctor, because we are at a bit of a loss explaining what we found at the crash site."

Her eyes darted to the left, avoiding his. He nodded. She knew what he meant, knew something unusual had been found out there in the woods.

David left the room, clenching his teeth. She was sexy as hell, and she was involved in something. Had there been special cargo? Did she know why her jet had been shot down? Who had done it, or, if the jet had failed, why? It occurred to him that it was possible she had two missions on the base, *possible* her assignment with his team might be just a cover. After all, his upcoming assignment had been so secret that he barely knew more than the basics. She might be something a lot more complicated than a psychtech. The urge to bang his head against the corridor wall was difficult to ignore. *I don't need this. Hell, nothing is ever simple anymore.*

He paced down the corridor toward the base's chemical-testing facilities. Probably it was none of his business. He should concentrate on getting his team through this last round of tests and getting them up there, into space. But it rubbed at him, bothered him the way she'd lied so badly. If she were simply a psychtech, why hide the truth?

The questions gnawed at him until he reached the test lab. Here, he might get some answers, even if it wasn't his business. Branscombe had a contact in the labs and had promised him some answers on the samples they'd collected at the crash site.

David tapped his compad, now hooked to his uniform shirt collar instead of the flak helmet he'd worn earlier. "Brown here. Branscombe, do you have any results? I'm outside lab one."

The door slid open. Branscombe nodded at him. She sat on a stool, her long lanky frame crowding a young man in a lab coat as she observed his work. "Lab rat here says something's wrong with our samples."

"What do you mean?" David strode into the room and stared at the tall, thin man clicking buttons on gear he'd never laid eyes on before.

"You guys have got to go." The labtech flicked his eyes up at David and then back to his work. "You shouldn't be here at all. This lab is off limits."

"What's the problem, Harry?" Branscombe cajoled. "You were okay with me being here a few minutes ago."

"This stuff…" Harry poked at the sample bag of dirt sitting on the counter beside his machinery, "this stuff is not a known polymer. It shouldn't even exist."

David picked up the bag. It looked like a bag of dirt. None of the strange melted plastic appeared to be inside, at least not to the naked eye. "Explain."

"It's like nothing I can identify. The comp is spitting out red flags all over the place. I've already received instructions to keep silent and report every person aware of this sample. This is bad." The labtech ran his fingers through his already wild hair, explaining why every strand seemed styled to stand on end.

David set the bag gingerly down on the table. He looked at Branscombe and found the unflappable captain's eyebrows had almost hit her hairline. "Report to whom, Harry?" David demanded.

The labtech looked miserably up at him. "I don't know. The security level is so high I can't even access the sender."

ALINNA SLID out from between the sheets on the medtech bed and put her bare feet against the coolness of the floor tiles. The halls of the facility remained quiet and empty. Her stomach grumbled, the only sound in the stillness of the early evening. Her internal command unit indicated the Earth hour of oh-two-hundred, and she was starving. Her mouth twisted. Perhaps hiding out here and studying the Humans wasn't going to be such a great idea. The cover was perfect. Her initial research on the subject of "psychtech" indicated she would have the opportunity to study the newest Human flight team's emotional stability until she was clear on every nuance. But the food…the food she'd experienced so far was simply disgusting, nothing but nutrient-enriched mush. She hadn't been able to stomach more than a single bite.

She had to concentrate on her successes. She'd been able to link her internal command unit to the system on the Human base long enough to change the records of Dr. Janet MacPherson so that they now bore her picture. She'd read through the dead doctor's background, all the while blessing the lost woman's *Lin'thal,* her soul. It went against Inarrii custom to disturb the dead, but she hoped the woman wouldn't mind loaning her identity for a short while. The Inarrii were here to help the Humans as much as themselves, to offer them the protection and support of the huge Confederacy in exchange for some of the Human solar system's material resources, and for a partnership between the peoples. Surely the dead doctor's soul would find comfort in that.

Now, Alinna was prepared. She understood what Starforce would be expecting of her in terms of the psychological tests she would have to use to evaluate the new team. As long as no one looked too closely, she would pass as MacPherson. It was just very lucky she hadn't needed a blood transfusion when she was injured, because she seriously doubted there would be a match for her on Earth.

Her stomach rumbled again. *It's hard to concentrate on the good things when you're starving.*

She scanned the building. Very few people were in the medical facility, let alone awake and alert. She stepped across the room to the door and peeked outside. No one. Passing through the doorway, she silently crossed the hall to a set of lockers. She'd made note of them when the young medtech had showed her the cleansing facilities. The novelty of the water shower had been pure delight to her overloaded *L'inar* and had given her at least a little sensory relief. She'd been space-bound for over a year, and water for more than drinking seemed like an amazing luxury. Shipboard water could never be used in such a way, but the ultra-sonic showers on her ship were not without their comforts.

She flipped the door to the first locker open. Nothing. A second cabinet revealed only linens, but she grinned in relief as she opened the third. In a clear bag, she found her emergency pouch and her favorite wristlet, which until this moment she hadn't even noticed was gone. There was simply too much happening, too much pressure. She hadn't even tried to contact command to let them know she was alive and had assumed a Human identity. A ten-second burst of verbal message might make it through without detection, but it was a huge risk. Alinna glanced up and down the hall. She quietly took out the bag with her belongings and shut the locker door. Stepping silently, she slipped back into her room and sat down on the bed with a sigh of relief.

She ran her finger over the *tocuh* seal on the pouch and quickly flipped through the contents until she found what she was looking for. Her stomach rumbled again. Gripping the plastic packet, she looked up at a small sound. Major David Brown leaned against the door frame in the entrance to her room. His muscular arms crossed over his chest, and he stared unsmiling at her, his dark blue eyes appearing black in the dim night-lights.

Alinna sucked in a breath, her heart seeming to skip its regular beat. Startled, she blurted the first thing she could think of. "Do you have any idea how bad the food is here?"

"Is that what you've got there, a little snack?" He stepped closer to the bed.

She gripped the emergency pouch a little tighter to her body as her mind raced through the list of its contents. Exactly what had she stuffed in there the last time she'd updated the boring Confederacy-issued contents? She couldn't remember. She set the pouch aside, pretending disinterest, and peeled the wrapper off the nutria-bar she had located before the major's unexpected arrival. "It isn't much, but it's a lot better than what they served for supper."

Major Brown's eyes never left hers, but as she took a bite of the dried snack, a small smile caught at the corners of his mouth. "I have to admit that the slop they serve here in the medlab is the worst I've ever experienced. No flavorings, and nothing to chew."

Alinna shivered again. Her feet were cold from the touch of the bare floors, but it was his proximity that caused her reaction. She turned, swung her legs up onto the bed and moved the emergency pouch to the bedside table on the opposite side of the room from the curious officer. He watched her every move, and she noted with interest that his eyes lingered longer on her legs than on the emergency pouch. She pulled the cover up over her feet.

"Can I help you with something?"

"No." He moved closer, reached for the pitcher of water the medtech had left on the suspended bedtable. He poured her a drink and offered it to her.

"Thank you." She immediately took a sip, relieved at the distraction. It was clear he suspected her of something, or at the very least distrusted her. This could be a result of her cover position—her research had revealed that psychtechs were not always welcomed in the military forces.

"Unless there is something you'd like to tell me about your real mission here."

Alinna choked on the water. *He knows!* "Excuse me?"

Major Brown reached out for her hands, steadying the glass of water threatening to spill in her shaking grip. His skin felt cool to the touch, much cooler than Inarrii skin, and rougher, the texture mesmerizing. Tiny golden hairs caught the light on the pale skin of his forearms, dotted with the strange dots of his freckles. His glare softened as he looked into her eyes. "I don't know exactly what's going on, *Dr. MacPherson*, but something isn't right. I can't risk the upcoming mission when I don't have everyone using the same playbook." He looked deeper into her eyes, looked straight into her *Lin'thal*. "I don't know what you've got yourself involved in, but if you'll tell me, I'll help you as best I can."

"I'm not involved in anything, but I am very tired." She pulled away from his touch and set the glass of water down near her emergency pouch. Hardening the tone of her voice, she added a slight empathic push to her words. "I would like to rest now."

A muscle jumped along the major's jaw line. A wave of resentment rolled from his psyche, but he turned away and headed for the door. She sagged back against the raised mattress of her bed in relief, until he glanced back at her. A shadow from the doorway fell across his face, but she didn't need to see him to recognize his intent.

"I'll see you in the morning then, *Doctor*."

She recognized his emotional focus. Like a wild game hunter on her homeworld, he'd targeted her, and she knew he had no intention of letting her get away.

Chapter 3

Alinna tossed and turned on the narrow medlab bed. The hateful covers alternated their mindless form of torture: first binding her down, stifling her with their unfamiliar weight, only to have her shivering in the cool night air and grasping for them when she threw them off. She thought longingly about her wide mattress on board the ship she'd left hidden on the dark side of the moon, with its heated air covers and the soft recorded sounds of home.

Sleep eluded her. She shook her head at the impossibility of being able to rest after Major Brown had practically accused her of being an imposter and then offered to help. If he knew the truth of what she was and why she was here, there would be no offer of rescue. From what she had heard of his upcoming mission, the team being assembled on the base was to be the major defense force for a covey of settlers headed for Mars. What else would they be defending those people from, but aliens?

Alinna gritted her teeth. The stress was getting to her. There were lots of things the Humans needed to protect themselves against in space, but neither the Inarrii, nor the

Confederacy, were one of them. The Confederacy needed resource-rich planets, and people to work them, but unlike some, they didn't believe in taking what wasn't theirs.

Alinna rubbed her hands over her forearms, stroking the leading edge of her *L'inar* nerve lines. She wet her lips with her tongue. An ache was forming in her core, one that had gone unsatisfied for so long that it was unnatural. Inarrii were not meant to be alone. They needed companionship and sex to keep sane, especially in high-stress situations. She grimaced. *I couldn't be any more stressed unless I was under fire.*

She closed her eyes and looked with her empathic senses, searching for a lover who could not exist among the Humans. It was a fruitless search, and she knew it, but her body was crying out for release and her mind following suit.

The medlab lay quiet around her. As her psyche wandered, she encountered only a few alert minds. Her thoughts returned to the confusing offer made by Major David Brown. The big male could not know what kind of help she would most like at this point. Finally, among the sleeping minds on the base, she found his presence—much brighter than she would have expected. She looked closer, her mind grazing across his, expecting to sense the flow of muted emotion that ruled a subconscious mind. Instead bright, focused passion flooded her. Immediately she was swept inside.

Alinna gasped as David's lips found hers. She struggled to pull away, shocked at the intensity of the sensation. The major was experiencing a vivid dream, and she could sense every nuance. This had never happened before; her talents had always stopped at the empathic level, and she'd chosen partners with the same level of ability. But here, she could feel his touch, see every detail, even smell his spicy cologne.

David's mind held on to her psyche, his desire a leash that wound around her and held her tight. As if he realized he had caught her within his dream, his mind pulled hers into a close embrace. His dream body molded itself to hers. She could feel the outline of his hardened muscles through his uniform, and her heart leapt with desire.

"So, you want me to call you Alinna."

Alinna stiffened, this shock even greater than the last. There was no indication on the species evaluation to indicate Humans had any sort of psychic ability, but clearly they were wrong. The man had just spoken to her mentally, albeit in a dream.

"If I call you Alinna, what will you call me?"

His mental voice rubbed against her in the same way his deep-toned speech did in the physical world. It resonated with sexual promises, no matter what the words communicated. She relaxed against him and felt his grip loosen in kind. This was a dream to him, a sexual dream. She felt her own desire return with its familiar ache. She smiled. She wasn't one to put aside an opportunity like this. She'd figure out how he came to have these abilities later, but for now she'd make this the best dream he'd ever had.

"David, of course," she purred against him, leaning into his embrace to rest her lips against the pulse in his throat. Her empathic senses felt his desire leap at her response, and she stoked his fires, pouring heat into his emotional hearth. She dragged her fingers down his arms, tracing patterns on his naked skin where *L'inar* would be, were he Inarrii, with the edge of her fingernails.

"I wouldn't call you Alinna. I'd call you sweetness, my sexy sweet thing."

She felt her eyebrows climb. No one had ever given her a lover's name. She rubbed against him, letting the image of her medlab gown that had followed her psyche into his dream fade away. Naked, she rubbed as much of her skin against his as she could, beginning a dance she prayed would last the rest of the night and soothe her stressed senses. Slowly she cupped the bulge in his pants with one hand and sighed in delight. He was Inarrii-sized everywhere.

"Naughty." He gripped her hands within his and held them captive as he kissed her, probing the opening between her lips with his tongue.

Alinna moaned into his mouth, writhing against him. Her desire overwhelmed her, pushing her to rush into a deeper intimacy without savoring the slow burn he created within her.

"I want you! I need…"

"I know, sweetness, shhh." Holding her wrists tight with one hand, he slid his other down to caress her skin, stroking the *L'inar* wrapping in curls around her breasts until she whimpered. He paused in his caresses, staring at the nerve lines that were sending waves of pleasure to her core. She felt the moisture in her *sinaa* well pooling, her heat growing. It was possible he would bring her to orgasm just staring at her. She needed this so badly.

"Your tattoos, your tattoos remind me…" He frowned.

"They remind you of how sexy I am, how different and desirable." She broke in, pushing at him empathically to remember only how much he wanted her now, not how he suspected her in the conscious world. If he stopped now, she might die from sheer frustration.

He looked into her eyes.

"You are different. And hot. I want to fuck you so hard, you'll feel it in the morning, even if this is just a dream."

She gasped. He was aware of the dream. Before she could accept the ramifications of that, he was cupping her breast again, drawing his lips down to suck at her taut nipple. She shuddered, arching into him. Each touch brought a response, an increase in the urgency she was feeling to the point that she clung to him when he let her hands go to explore the curving *L'inar* across her belly.

David dropped to his knees to kneel in front of her, his shirt disappearing as her medtech shift had. Another example of his control over his dream, but one she didn't care to reflect on at the moment. Instead she stroked his hair, marveled at his smooth skin. An Inarrii male would have been covered in ridges by now, his desire clearly visible as the reddish *L'inar* reacted to his arousal. Part of her desired to touch him and tease him in a vain effort to stimulate a reaction that wasn't possible.

"Your skin is so soft. I think I love your tattoos. They point me in the right direction."

David pulled her down to him, cradling her in his arms for a moment before he settled her on her back on the soft floor. He ran his fingers lightly over the curling nerves blatantly displayed on her skin. She arched and moaned in his hands. When he began to lick the lines, follow their coils with his tongue down the curve of her hip, she moaned louder and opened her knees for him. With each sweep of his fingers or tongue, she felt pleasure winding through her body, focusing her attention on the heat in her sex. He cupped her ass cheeks in his hands and squeezed, lifting her hips to display the *L'inar* on her inner thighs.

Alinna knew she should stop him. Stroking her *L'inar* this way, doing this meant something. But her mind buzzed with arousal she could no longer control. It had been too long since her last true release. Everything seemed a bit cloudy, fuzzy on the edges as he traced the twisting designs with his tongue. *There is something he is doing…something he shouldn't do…*but her mind darkened as his mouth wound along the *L'inar* on her inner thigh until he grazed her sex —her *sinaa*—and his tongue flicked out to part the swollen lips there. She could only focus on the sensation as he delved into her core, licking and sucking, pulling her up to a pinnacle of pleasure so steep that she let out a short scream and toppled over.

Waves of pleasure swamped her psyche in a way she'd never before experienced. Her orgasm rocked within her, but he didn't stop as he pushed her legs farther apart and knelt between them. His pants melted away in the dreamscape to expose his thick cock, its jutting length so different than the Inarrii males she was used to, perhaps not as long, but so smooth and very thick. He didn't wait for her orgasm to subside but pushed within her, slowly, each stroke parting her further as he planted himself deeper within her *sinaa.*

"Ya'sai lenali!" she gasped.

"What?" He hesitated, but she grabbed his hips, pulling him down until the base of his cock pressed against her.

"More, lover! Just…more."

David pulled back, and she moaned at the unfamiliar feeling. He was so much wider than an Inarrii, and it felt… good. The sensation was as though he was splitting her in two, but she wanted it, wanted it so badly she pulled at his hips, urging him to stroke faster.

He nipped her neck in return, growling at her. *"Go easy, sweetness."* He tweaked one of her nipples, and she whimpered, the flash of sensation sizzling through her *L'inar.* Another orgasm was building; the warm glow from the last was not yet gone, and yet her body creamed against his invading cock, welcoming it and the pleasure he brought. She wrapped her arms and legs around him. As if he knew what she desired, he knelt up, pulling her with him until he stood. He held her weight easily, although she took some of it by clinging to his shoulders and rocked her hips against his.

David kissed her, his lips hot with passion, his tongue mating with hers. He cupped her ass again as they rocked, and she shuddered, feeling his desire to possess her, to take her body and soul, and keep her in a way that felt like forever. He fucked her now with his tongue and cock, and she returned her delight at the feeling and her acceptance to him in an empathic wave, flooding his senses with the same pleasure she felt.

The exchange of sensation and emotion rippled back and forth between them, growing as they experienced each other's reactions. She sensed his orgasm. He pumped his seed within her, just as an Inarrii male would have done. She shuddered along with him, the sensations so intense she found blackness engulfing her.

PANIC SEIZED David as he thrashed awake. His sheets were drenched with his sweat and cum. With a groan, he disentangled himself from the wet material and rubbed a hand across his eyes. He slapped his hands down on the bed. *What an idiot.* He'd panicked because he'd lost her, a dream girl. Granted, it had definitely been the most vivid dream he'd ever had, but a man shouldn't be desperate for a woman after a single fuck, not even a perfect dream woman. The sense of loss he felt was completely unwarranted. Maybe he did need a psychtech, but it had better not be Dr. Janet MacPherson—Alinna. She would not understand his apparent need to fuck her silly in his dreams.

He slumped back on the bed, only to grumble and stand up. The mattress was soaked. He must have pumped a bucket of cum in his sleep. For once, he blessed the size of the base's small staff. Because of the limited number of people on the large base, he had a good-sized room to himself with its own bathroom and could go directly to the shower, no matter what time, no questions asked. He ripped the sheets from the bed as he moved, tossing them in the wash chute near the washroom door. He always slept naked now that he had the privilege of privacy. He stepped into the shower unit and flicked on the hot water. A pressure spray streamed down on him, rinsing him clean and washing the last of the adrenalin from his system.

He leaned his face into the flow of water. Hot streams of liquid poured over his face and down his chest. He'd enjoy this now, while he could. If all went well, he'd be living in space for an extended amount of time. Water would be limited and certainly not for use in bathing. He tilted his head down to allow the water to pour down the back of his neck and shoulders. God only knew how he'd smell after a months of sponge wipes instead of a shower.

Thinking about something trivial wasn't helping. His mind drifted back to his dream, to how incredible Alinna looked nude, wearing only those mind-blowing tattoos. *I wonder if they really do curve around her body like that. Hell, I wonder if she's as hot as that.* Even her skin had been hot to the touch. But all he had to go on in the real world was the shapeless medical gown and the edge of a cultural tat. No way to know if the marks really curled around her breast or decorated her thighs all the way to her pussy. His cock swelled at the thought. He snorted at himself. *Get a grip. You'll never know. Besides, only in a dream does a woman respond like that.* In his dream she had given herself over completely do him. That just didn't happen in the real world.

With a groan, he shut the water off. He didn't need to be thinking about fucking the psychtech, if that was even what she was. He'd already overstepped his bounds, privately investigating material from the crash site. That was definitely someone else's job. If his curiosity raised enough red flags, there'd be no way he'd be assigned to lead the team on a permanent basis. He had to get things back on track.

David stepped out of the shower and checked the vid. Eight hundred hours. Too early to meet with the psychtech and get her moved out of the medlab. She'd probably be going through her release forms right now. He stopped, staring at himself in the mirror. Perhaps now *would* be a good time to go and meet her, listen to the answers she gave to the medtechs as they went through her medical record and she retrieved her belongings. Then there was the matter of that strange little sack...

David slapped his hand down on the counter. He had to get it together, get back to his mission. He had no business being curious; curiosity killed the promotion if not the cat. He just had to get the woman checked into her lab and set up so she could run her tests, pass him and his team on these final fucking evals. *Get through it. Pass the test, get assigned, lead!* He ran a hand through his spiky hair. A flick of a switch, and his laser exfoliator took care of the shadow on his jaw line. Moving with brusque efficiency, he strode to his room and pulled on a fresh uniform. The sight of his stripped bed had his cock hardening again. He gritted his teeth in frustration. Wet dreams like a teenager and he still wanted more. Moments later, he was striding down the hall toward the medlab.

"Branscombe to Brown, requesting secure channel." The hail came across David's compad. David tapped the pad and switched over to the sub-vocal communicator imbedded in his ear and vocal cords. No one passing by would hear him as he spoke with his captain.

"Brown here."

"My little lab rat pal here has traced those red flags. I don't think we have much to worry about there. The flags are coming from the You-fo Squad."

The so-called You-fo Squad was a small branch of Starforce Intelligence Department that regularly investigated possible alien incursions on Earth—given their nickname because they were looking for little green men and their UFOs. At least, that was one version of the meaning. Personally, David thought the name could stand for the fact that to land in that division meant "you fucked-up." No one took them seriously. There hadn't been a proven instance of any alien activity in the universe, let alone Earth, in the centuries Humans had been venturing into space. Even his team, a force meant to defend the space settlers, wasn't expecting to defend them against aliens. The only real danger in space was another group of Humans. David felt some of the tension in his shoulders ease.

"Gotcha." But something wasn't right. "So why the secure channel?"

"I took the liberty of reviewing our survivor's records," Branscombe hedged.

David shook his head, ignoring a curious stare from a group of enlisted personnel as he strode down the hallway toward the medlab. Branscombe took chances and bucked the system. That was the real reason she was still a captain and hadn't moved up in the ranks, despite her length of service and her piloting skill.

"I don't want to know, Captain."

"Oh, yes you do, Major."

David hit the corridor leading to the medical facilities. He hesitated, seeing Dr. MacPherson—Alinna—standing with two of the medtechs at the admin desk. They appeared deep in conversation.

"What do you have?" he growled into the com.

"Well, unless she's been taking some serious growth hormone, the woman we found isn't Janet MacPherson."

Chapter 4

Alinna felt a wave of hot emotion slap against her before she saw him. David pulsed with anger. The power of his fury forced her to take a step back as he approached, yet he barely glanced at her as he greeted the medtechs with a smile.

"Is our patient ready to go, then?" he asked the tech behind the counter. His voice was calm, belying the feelings she sensed from him.

Alinna reached out with her empathic senses. The anger was there, fiery to her psychic touch, and definitely directed toward her. She suppressed a shudder. Had he realized his dream last night had been more than a dream? He'd shown more awareness than she'd thought possible in one untrained in psychic powers. Had he guessed she'd imposed herself into his fantasy? Not that she'd actually *meant* to invade the dream. She'd been pulled in by him. But she could have stopped it. Although his powers were strong enough to envelope hers, his strength couldn't match her training.

Perhaps David felt she'd invaded his privacy. She

grimaced. Such an invasion, if it had been on purpose, was Inarrii taboo. But David was Human and would have no such aversion. Thoughts raced through Alinna's mind. Even in his dream, David has sensed something was off, despite her pushes to ignore his suspicions and focus on his lust. Perhaps he'd realized she wasn't Human. A ripple ran across her *L'inar* nerve lines, and she fought to control the panicked reaction.

David turned his gaze to her, his eyes cold. She swallowed hard.

"Let's go, *Dr. MacPherson.* Your lab is waiting."

David's voice lacked any of the warmth of last night. Alinna missed the soft way he'd called her "sweetness." He'd held her and kissed her like she meant something to him, and his psyche had reveled when she'd given in to his control, surrendered her body to his desires and pace. But today, he was fire and ice, not the languid heat of sex or caring. Alinna swallowed her shock at his anger and watched him carefully. Surely if he suspected she was anything other than Human, she'd be under arrest right now.

"After you." David gestured down the hallway and gave her a wide smile, one that didn't reach his eyes. The medtechs laughed, their psyches emoting mild amusement at his apparent flirtation. Alinna was anything but amused as she moved ahead of David. She could feel his cool gaze on the back of her neck and thanked the gods she had left her hair long enough to cover her *L'inar.* She couldn't completely hide them, but between her free-hanging locks and the high collar of the Starforce suit, the majority of her nerve lines were safe from casual inspection. Alinna fought the urge to hunch down within her collar. David's presence behind her felt far from casual. She needed to distract him and disarm his anger as quickly as possible.

She hesitated as the corridor split in two directions. David brushed past her to take the lead.

"I'm sure you will want to rest. I'll take you to your quarters first." The brusque tone in his voice finally revealed his inner turmoil.

"But I thought you said my lab was waiting for me. I really don't want to rest anymore. I've had enough of that at the medlab."

"I'm sure your lab can wait. If you don't want to rest, you must have other things you need to…accomplish." He glanced at her, his deep blue eyes holding her gaze as though he was waiting for her to reveal something to him.

"No…" She stumbled over the word. Lying to him made her stomach twist. "No. I'm sure you want to get started on the psych tests for you and your pilots. I understand deployment of your team is being delayed until I issue a final release."

David stopped, turning back to clutch her elbow. "So you're going ahead with the tests?"

"Of…of course I am."

His eyes searched hers. She wondered, as she marveled at the bright blue eye-color that would never occur naturally in her people, what he could be looking for. She reached out, using her senses to touch his psyche. Anger, confusion, distrust, lust. His feelings surrounded her, boiling like gas bubbles in a hydroponics web. She probed deeper, looking for the source of his feelings. Her empathic touch recoiled as it ran into a rough wall within him. The implications of the wall burned through her thoughts. He had a block, something she hadn't felt within him last night. He'd obviously built it himself in reaction to his distrust. *How did he learn to do that?*

David let go of her elbow as though it burned his fingertips. Whatever he'd looked for within her eyes appeared to remain elusive. His eyebrows drew together, and his lips tightened. Even as a scowl marred his face, Alinna reveled in the beautifully masculine curve of his jaw. Pleasure ran from the *L'inar* lacing the inner edge of her elbow where he'd gripped her. Even an aggressive touch from him reminded her of the release she'd felt last night, and of how she'd like to feel it again.

David turned away, striding once again down a long barren corridor of the Starforce building. Alinna stared at his back for a moment and then followed. Whatever was wrong, whatever he suspected, she couldn't reach it by looking within his emotions. She stiffened her back and marched after him. For now, she'd follow his lead, and she'd do her duty. By running those tests, she'd find out far more about the Human species than she ever would by watching them from the safe distance of the spy shuttle.

A few moments and several turns later, Alinna found herself following David outside of the building. David strode on, so she continued to follow him. She shaded her eyes from the bright sun. Although the yellow star reminded her of home, the blue skies on Earth were nothing like her own planet's red heavens. David turned away from the buildings and led her to an open field. Behind him, she could see the gates to the hangar storing the newly built Star ships destined for his squadron. The Inarrii were well aware of the Humans' new ships and their technical aspects. That wasn't what she'd been sent to study, but their unusual shape caught her attention.

When David stopped suddenly, she nearly stumbled into him. Catching her balance, she looked up into his amazing eyes.

"Why are you here?" he demanded.

"What...what do you mean?"

"Cut the crap. I know you're not Dr. Janet McPherson.

41

I don't know who the hell you are. But no one can hear you out here, and I want some answers. Because I sure as hell am not going to sit there while you do some crazy pretend psych test and risk putting my team out of the running for the next security mission." David gripped her upper arms and pulled her closer to him. She could feel the outline of his fingers as they pressed into her skin through the material of her borrowed Starforce uniform. The touch, while not gentle, quickened her desire as he pressed against her *L'inar* nerves.

Alinna fought to keep her longing in check. Her lips parted, and her tongue darted out to moisten their suddenly dry surface. Part of her wanted to tell him the truth. Lying felt wrong, foreign, and completely against Inarrii custom. But she had a duty to perform. Before she could lie again, he interrupted her.

"I don't want to hear another story. Maybe you can't tell me the truth, but we both know you aren't who you're pretending to be." David let go of her and paced a few steps away. He turned his back to her. "You've altered the records, but not far enough back. If anyone else had been looking, they wouldn't have noticed the inconsistencies. But my captain is former Starforce Security. Clearly, you have the clearance to change those records and they're top-class Starforce docs. There's no way to make those changes unless you have authorization from security level nine. But you aren't Dr. MacPherson."

He turned back to look at her, his hot gaze running the length of her body. "You look nothing like her, by the way."

Shock kept Alinna silent. His suspicions were so close to the truth. All he needed was to take one further step, to imagine her not within his own organization but a spy from without, and her cover would be completely blown. If she were taken into custody and investigated, it would only be a matter of time before they discovered she wasn't Human. Anxiety forced her heartbeat into a rapid patter. She wasn't trained for the possibility of capture, but she'd known it was a risk when she took this path.

SHE JUST STOOD THERE, looking like the sex kitten from his wet dream last night. A minute crawled by. She didn't deny his accusations, but she didn't say he was right, either. For an instant, he wondered if he'd made a mistake. If she really was a Starforce spy, he'd blown her cover. A breeze flitted between them, its light kiss lifting her hair away from the back of her neck. He caught a glimpse of the edge of her neck tattoo and swallowed hard. If she was what he suspected, Starforce Intelligence, then she was here for a reason. Blowing her cover could be as dangerous to his career as following his instinct to press his lips to her neck and follow that tattoo wherever it led.

"What else do you know?" Alinna finally spoke. Her soft voice shook, and he noticed the way her eyes darted past the ship hangars and across the empty field, as though looking for escape.

At that moment, David knew he could never let her go. He wanted her nearby for a number of reasons, not the least of which was how frightened she looked. He needed those psych tests done, needed her approval for his team to accept the mission. And now, he needed to find out the truth. He couldn't let it go. She was scared and obviously out of her depth. She might be a Starforce spy, but something was seriously wrong. Her vulnerability hit him like a punch to the gut.

The woman he'd fucked in his dreams last night feared

for her life today. No other worry could put that look in a person's eyes—desperation.

"I know the You-fos are pretty interested in something we found at the crash site." David watched her closely. Her eyes flicked to glance around the field, as they had when he'd questioned her in the medlab. She knew exactly what he was talking about. He watched the pulse at the base of her throat jump, and blinked as the tattoo on the edge of her hairline seemed to move. He swallowed hard. *Focus.*

"What? What is it, Alinna? That is your real name, isn't it?"

She took a deep breath. "I think we'd better go to the lab. Start the psych tests." She caught his gaze, held it. "I don't know what You-fos are, and I don't care. I'm here to do a job, and it's a job you need done, as well. So let me do my duty."

David ground his teeth together, but something told him he wouldn't be getting any more from her right now.

"Let's go, then." He let her step past him, then caught her gently by the elbow, swinging her around to face him. "But, we're not done with this."

"We are, Major, if you want to see your pilots in space."

She had him there. He needed her to conduct those tests, whether she was qualified to do so or not. As long as he didn't reveal her true identity, or lack thereof, she could still give his team the green light to go. They deserved the chance to prove themselves in space and were the best option for the job. He believed it, knew it with everything inside him. They didn't need another set of tests other than to satisfy some clerk pushing red tape.

He let go of her, although the urge to pull her closer and end the argument the way he really wanted to was strong. She had the control now, but he'd dearly like to take it back, take her in his arms and kiss her into submission. She'd ignored his offer for help last night, just like she was pushing him away now. She needed him but wouldn't admit it, yet. Whatever was going on—the crash of her jet, the strange material at the crash site, her stolen identity— she needed him. And he'd be there for her, if he could. If it didn't mean getting benched and stuck on Earth. And even then… He shook his head at the thought. What had she done to him in just a day?

David led the way back into the building. Inside the base, there was no privacy. It was the Starforce way. Almost every conversation would be recorded somewhere. Alinna followed him slowly. He looked back at her as he reached the doorway. She limped slightly, each step appearing to inflict a flash of pain.

"Is the wound on your leg still bothering you?"

"Let's just get to the lab, Major."

"The medtechs said you were good to go." He heard the accusation in his voice. *Damn.* He wanted to help her, but she was determined not to let him anywhere near, shaking her head at his concern.

"Fine." He reached toward the side of the door to pass his secur-ident over the monitor, but she slammed into the door before he had a chance. He reached out to steady her, his shock mirroring hers.

"You aren't okay."

"It didn't open."

"No…" He stared at her. "This is a secure exit. You need a pass." He showed her the chip in his wrist unit. He considered the quick way her eyes darted to his wrist and back to the door. The technology couldn't be new to her; perhaps it was old? "Did you have something different?" He fished for information. Where was she from? What division didn't bother with secure passes?

45

"Open the door, David." She glared at him, clearly aware he was looking for more.

A flash of interest raced down David's body. The way she said his name, tinted with desperation, was with the exact inflection as she'd used in his dream last night. Just a hint of an accent he couldn't place, and only appeared when she wasn't focused. Slowly he passed his wrist unit over the scanner. The door slid open, and she pushed inside, her limp disguised but still apparent to his watchful eyes.

He took his time as they walked to the lab. He didn't want to rush for a couple of reasons. One, she really shouldn't be walking if her leg hurt that much. Two, the sooner they were at the lab, the sooner she would start the psych tests. All the members of his team had to pass, or they wouldn't get the sanction to begin the security mission to escort the new settlers. So he wouldn't be alone with Alinna, wouldn't find out more about what she was really doing. Wouldn't get to stare at her hot body without someone in the team taking notice.

"Captain Branscombe to Major Brown." David's compad recorded the irritated sound of his second in command's voice with perfection. "Requesting a secure line."

David switched to the silent sub-vocal channel. "Brown here."

"Well? Did you tell her we know she's an imposter? What did she say?"

"She doesn't admit to anything, but there's something going on. She's in trouble."

"Great. Don't tell me she looked at you with those big green eyes and, immediately, you knew she needed you."

"I think you know you should stop right there." Anger swelled in David's chest, the taste of it bitter on his tongue.

"Report with officers Lee and Yancy to psychometrics lab three at ten hundred hours."

"Yes, sir. One final note, sir." Cynicism was one of Branscombe's more annoying talents. "The You-fos are expected to arrive in two days' time to investigate the findings on the crash site."

"Let them. All we did was find the stuff. We're going to live and let live, Captain. By then, the tests should be finished, and we'll be waiting on our assignment."

"I see. Branscombe out." She still sounded annoyed, but he could tell she understood his intent—he was going to get the team through the psych evals, whether Alinna was a registered psychtech or not.

David looked at Alinna. "You'll be working from psychometrics lab three. It's coded to your voice. They registered it at the medlab." He stopped at the doorway to her new office. "Just speak your name into the scanner."

"Thank you. Ten hundred hours sounds good to me, as well. Thank you for asking your captain and the others to attend at that time."

Alinna didn't look at him while she spoke, and he was grateful, for she would have glimpsed the confusion and shock on his face. *How the hell did she hear me on a sub-vocal channel? She's got to have some serious spy tech.* He scanned her body. He'd love to know where she could be hiding any spy gadgets in her tight little uniform.

"Dr. Janet MacPherson." Alinna spoke the name into the scanner.

David shook his head. How could she have made it so far into the spy ranks if her voice shook when she uttered her alias? "Fine. Captain Branscombe and two others will be here today. I'll report to you tomorrow with the rest of the team." He turned away from her as she stepped into her office. The urge to stay with her was strong, as was the urge to push her into admitting what was wrong do he could help. He wanted his team passed, but he wouldn't be able to ignore her obvious lies if she couldn't operate within the lab. If she was clearly untrained as a psychtech, he'd have to report her.

Chapter 5

Alinna sagged against the wall. Her body, her mind—everything—felt tired. The day seemed to have stretched on forever. She had performed her duty and discovered more about the Humans than even she had hoped for under these strange circumstances. She sank to the floor and lowered her head to hold it in her hands. Her temples throbbed. She was paying the price for the effort she was putting out for her people. Her stress level was too high, and there was no end in sight. She'd left David, her only hope for any kind of relief from the stress she was under, in the hallway that morning. His emotions had bubbled close to the surface—confusion, anger, frustration—but they were nothing in comparison to the nearly out-of-control emotions of his team.

Today, she'd examined two of David's pilots. Lee and Yancy had participated in Alinna's rescue, and their emotions constantly snapped and popped in nearly identical waves of concern and curiosity. Clearly they were aware that something was going on with her, although she got no sense of betrayal or anger from them. She'd run the tests required for their final approval for long-term space-flight, easily found on the simple psychtech database. They were similar to what the Inarrii required, examining things like the level of integrity each officer possessed, and how generous and tolerant they might be when working with someone of a different race or nationality. If she had been a real Human psychtech, she would have passed the officers quite readily. But the true answers to those questions and the emotions underlying their answers could only be judged by opening her empathic abilities to the fullest. No lying or hiding was possible from her at that level. This was invaluable information for her people. And that was where her personal cost had been applied. The mental toll of opening herself to these unshielded people was high. It was difficult to remain in control when she felt what they felt, and she knew they were holding back questions about her. These people were good, and even if she was doing it for a good reason, she was deceiving them.

Alinna needed a reprieve from the pounding of emotion against her senses. She hadn't been able to stomach trying another horrible Human meal after the slop at the medlab, and hunger was adding to her strain as her emergency rations were almost finished. To add to her misery, her leg *still* hurt.

But Captain Branscombe was waiting in the next room. Her emotions were more complex than the other two pilots. They rattled against Alinna's emotional barriers like angry *burra* beetles against a solar shield. Relentless. The captain *wanted* to talk to her. Wanted to question Alinna. Branscombe was eager and, somehow, her emotions held the quality of angry revenge.

Alinna straightened her spine, pulled back her shoulders. She had to get through this to complete her mission. If she could gather information from the entire team, it would be enough. Then she would manage, somehow, to get back to her people and make her report. Alinna rubbed her temples again. If she called too soon, she would risk exposure and possibly ruin the entire mission. If the Humans discovered they were being spied on, they wouldn't be happy to join in a treaty with the Inarrii. If she called too late…well that thought didn't bear thinking about as she would lose the last chance she had at redeeming herself.

She stood and walked to the entrance. The swarm of emotions on the other side of the door made her hesitate before opening it. Alinna rubbed her fingertips over the edge of the *L'inar* on her inner arms. Inarrii were not meant for this level of extended stress on their own, but she had to make it through these interviews. She had to return with enough information, or her career was ruined. She was in too deep now to turn back.

Alinna opened the door. Captain Branscombe immediately stood and smiled at her, but it was more of a baring of teeth than a genuine smile of welcome. Alinna tamped down on her mental shields. The woman buzzed with anger.

"Please come with me, Captain." Alinna waved toward the door to her inner office, then turned to walk toward it. Exposing her back to the pilot felt dangerous, and Alinna fought to keep calm, to keep her *L'inar* from tightening into their raised banners of instinctual fear.

"This series of tests is designed to last just over an hour, but we will then be pursuing a second level of the exam which should take about thirty minutes," Alinna explained over her shoulder as she walked to the monitor. She motioned to the examination bench. "Please have a seat, and we will start a sequence of baseline questions to align your response to the monitor."

"I've done a few of these. I know the drill."

"Drill?"

"The routine."

Alinna glanced over at the female pilot. Her irritated response to a simple statement said a lot about her feelings for the testing process in general, even if she didn't verbalize the strong resentment Alinna could feel emanating from her.

"You've had the level-five tests before."

"I imagine you already know the answer to that, *Doctor*."

Alinna's fingers flew over the controls, aligning the machine without the control questions. Her empathic skills were far more accurate than this machine, but it was amazing on a certain level that the Humans had come this far in analyzing the complicated Human psyche. Alinna made a mental note to read into the history of the development of the tool, and of the extensive programming it must require.

"It isn't in your medical files," Alinna replied calmly.

"No, but I'm certain it's in my security files."

Alinna nodded. "I'm sure it is." She turned away and took a seat at her console. Her calm answers only seemed to infuriate the captain further. While this wreaked havoc on the level of stress Alinna was shunting away from her shields, the contrasting reaction would make a very interesting study—perhaps even a vital study of Human reaction for her people.

"Let's begin." Alinna started the standard level-five questions. The captain responded grudgingly, and Alinna could feel her frustration rising. She wasn't surprised when the captain began speaking before Alinna'd had the chance to ask the next question.

"Yes, my family loves me and respects my choice to be

in Starforce. Now, how about I ask a question, *Doctor?* How about you tell me just who you are?"

Alinna's thoughts raced. Captain Branscombe was obviously the source of information David had referred to when he said he knew Alinna was a spy. He and the captain clearly assumed she was on a clandestine mission, and that the psychtech position was her cover. *If they only knew how close to the truth they really were, and how wrong.*

"I think you know who I am. Let's return to the test. After all, you do need to complete this for your mission." Alinna kept any emotion from her voice. Lying was hard, so she would let the woman make her own assumptions. Even that deception churned her stomach. She returned to the set questions. "Are you proud to be a Starforce pilot?"

It was a trick question. They all were, even the ones she had designed to measure the Human reactions to possible interaction with another intelligent species.

The captain stared at her for a moment. Her cheeks flushed red to the roots of her short cropped blond hair, and her emotions pounded out anger and resentment. Clearly she had an issue with the Security forces, or more particularly, with the undercover levels of Starforce Intelligence. How the captain handled the situation would be an interesting reflection on the Human ability to cope with frustrating situations.

"I'm prouder than I would be if I were a Starforce spy."

Alinna stiffened. Although she had expected something of the sort, the words struck her like a blow. She responded with a question on her own personal agenda. "Does it bother you to know there are things hidden from you? Hidden for your own good?"

Captain Branscombe stood suddenly, leaving the monitored bench to pace the room. "Nothing should be hidden.

Lies help no one." She turned to face Alinna. "I understand that sometimes information is passed on from one level to another on a need-to-know basis, but I don't think most people want that. Most people…I…don't want or need that."

"Some information, if generally released, could prove to be dangerous to individuals or sometimes even to an entire population." Alinna put aside the controls for the test equipment. She felt uncomfortable with Captain Branscombe standing above her, so she stood too, her Inarrii height putting her at an advantage over the angry young woman. Since the anger didn't seem violent, she pushed harder. "Would you risk people's lives so that you could personally know about a covert mission?"

Captain Branscombe stared at her. She visibly ground her teeth. Then she turned away and sat down on the bench. "No. I wouldn't. Let's finish this damn test."

DAVID SAT on his bed and rubbed his face with his hands. The temptation to take a sleeping aid niggled at him. God knew the cool shower he'd taken hadn't helped either the fire in his loins or the tension in his mind. It was late, and he needed sleep. He'd spent the day going over the maintenance schedule for the new ships and worrying about his pilots undergoing the psych screens, while avoiding the psych lab all day. David grabbed the pillow and gave it a few half-hearted whacks. Thoughts of Alinna rolled around and around in his mind. Branscombe had assured him she was a high-level Starforce security officer—the way the files had been altered practically shouted it, along with the mysterious cargo on a Starforce airjet cleared for the top security base.

Unfortunately Alinna just didn't meet his understanding of a confident spy. She seemed lost, in trouble. Her vulnerability could be a calculated act to go along with her blatant sexuality and those magnificent eyes. She could be using all of these things to keep her cover clear or, now that it was blown, to keep him from reporting the discovery of her stolen identity. Of course, she also held the reins when it came to his career. He needed to make this next mission; it was the kind of opportunity that happened once in a lifetime. He deserved to go, his team was the best for the job, but without the final psych clearance, they weren't going anywhere.

David flopped back on the bed. If the woman wasn't so mysterious, and so pivotal to his career, he'd be tempted to hit on her. Those eyes, so fantastic, and her tattoos, they made him wild. Tomorrow, he'd ask her what they meant, and to hell with propriety. He closed his eyes. The way she'd looked at him so desperately, he wanted to help. He wanted to kiss her. Hell, he wanted to fuck her, screw her like he had in his dreams and make her forget whatever was wrong.

David slid a hand down to his already thickening cock. He flipped the elastic of his underwear back and stroked the length of his shaft and then gripped it in his fist. Her curves had been so sweet in his dream. He recalled the taste of her skin, the line of a tattoo as it curved in toward the sweet slope of her inner thigh. The image was so strong, he could taste her, feel her hot skin against his mouth.

"Please, David," her voice seemed to whisper in his ear as he fantasized about the mysterious woman.

"Sweetness…" He concentrated on the fantasy. It was as if she were right there with him. He kept his eyes closed.

"I need you," she begged, unconsciously echoing his earlier desire to help her.

Her hands touched him, stroked him. He could smell her mild female aroma of arousal. It was so real, he was tempted to open his eyes to check if she were really there in his room with him. Instead he kept them firmly closed so he could take the fantasy as far as he could.

"Be still, sweetness. I'll take care of you." He looked into her wide green eyes, so full with need. He took her lips with his, kissing her softly as he pulled her on top of him. Then he slowly invaded the heat of her mouth with his tongue. She moaned against him, her response to his implication immediate. She would surrender to him, allow him to take her in any way he wanted. She would give him the power to serve her the way he knew she needed.

He slid the fingers of one hand into her hair as he rolled over, taking her with him, pinning her naked body to the bed. Her fine locks slid against his skin, and he was surprised to see that the tattoos extended into her hairline from the base of her neck. Tattooing a scalp would have to hurt. Tomorrow, he would definitely ask her about her tats, but tonight, he would get to know each line in the most intimate of ways, even if it was only in his imagination.

He kissed her neck, sucking softly enough at her skin not to leave a bruise, but nipping lightly here and there. Her scent made his mouth water, a delicious aroma of musk and citrus encouraging him to savor the taste of her skin. Alinna writhed beneath him, spreading her knees to wrap her long legs around his torso. She ground her naked pussy against his hips, and he wished he'd taken a moment to remove his shorts.

With that thought, the material between them disappeared. David grinned. *Of course.* This was his fantasy; he could do any damn thing he pleased. The bed grew wider, giving him plenty of room to play with Alinna. She gasped, taking in the changes, especially the feeling of his thick cock now centered against her hot cunt. He kissed her before she could say a word. He tasted her, sucked lightly at her tongue and her lips. Citrus and woman, the heady flavor echoed the scent of her skin and hair. He could feel her pussy growing wetter beneath him. Finally, before he could lose control and plunge his cock inside her, he shifted to one side and dropped his body to the bed. She moaned, the sound low and vulnerable at his movement and turned toward him, keeping one leg over his hip, as though she never wanted him to leave her.

David ran the fingertips of his free hand down her body, skimming along her skin as he traced her curves to her nipple. He pinched the rosy bud, pulling at it until she rocked her hips against him in a silent plea. *A girl who had as many tattoos as Alinna would probably like a little rough play,* he thought. He moved his lips to her breast and sucked hard at her tight nipple. She threw back her head and groaned. David grinned, deciding he was right.

He levered himself up on his elbows to give himself the space he needed to reach her other breast and treated it to the same mild torture. As he suckled her, he slipped his hand down to stroke her pussy, delighted to find the naked skin there wet with her juices. He loved the fact that she had no soft curls of hair around her pussy, and marveled again at the way her tattoos extended in tendrils from her inner thighs all the way to these private inner lips.

"Tattoos here had to hurt like a bastard" he said silently to her as he traced their path with his wet fingers.

ALINNA GROANED in pleasure and in frustration. She

needed David—needed the release he could provide, the escape from all the tension of the mission. But he was surprising her again, both with his insight in how to please her and most importantly with his uncanny psychic abilities. He wasn't even asleep. This time, he had reached out to her mentally while fantasizing about her. He'd drawn her into his daydream, altered the physical limitations his mind had set upon it, and was now addressing her mentally, just as though he were born to the ability. Which she supposed he was, just not in the way the Inarrii expected a Human to be. Their species were far more similar than simple appearance.

Alinna gasped as David stroked her *sinaa*. She should be pulling away, should be escaping the base to find some way back to her people to make her report. What she now knew about the Humans was enough to finalize the decision on a direct approach by the Inarrii for a treaty, she was certain of that. But that would mean leaving David, an unappealing thought considering she wasn't even sure she could get home. Alinna's pulse raced as he stroked her again, slowly teasing open the folds of her *sinaa* until he could touch the center of her longing. He was the only thing keeping her from going insane on this lonely planet. She didn't want to leave David, and she certainly wasn't ending this now. She needed him.

With bold strokes, he brought her to the edge, so close to orgasm that she whimpered his name. Then he stopped, only to begin a slow exploration of her *L'inar* with his tongue down the length of her body. She breathed deeply, inhaling his scent. His cologne added a crisp touch of spice to his natural musk, much as an Inarrii male in heat's scent would. He was too slow, there was too much, and she needed more, now. She rocked against him as he mapped out every inch of her *L'inar* with his lips and tongue until he reached the innermost lines on her thighs. His skin was cool as he touched her, but his lips and tongue were hot, a surprising and delightful combination. He'd done this before, in the dream they had shared, and each touch of his hot tongue sent pulses of pleasure down her nerve lines.

Just as she was about to beg him to take her, she stiffened. He *had* done this before. She had allowed him to begin *M'itta lensahn*, the first step in the Inarrii mating ceremony, and she was allowing it *again*. Tracing her *L'inar* with his tongue marked her as his. If she let this continue, would they be mated? He had no *L'inar* nerve lines to taste and trace, so she couldn't have completed the ceremony, could she? Her mind raced back to the previous night.

"Oh fuck," she swore.

"Not yet." He laughed at her, looked up to meet her eyes. He must have caught her shocked look. "What's wrong?"

"We shouldn't do this…I don't really know you…" she trailed off as he lowered his mouth again to nuzzle the wet lips of her *sinaa*.

"You know me. And we both want this, need this." He spoke against her sex, the warm breath from his words teasing more pleasure from her throbbing core.

He was right about that. She did need him, and she could read his yearning as easily now as she had read his honest desire to help her earlier. They were two different species; surely she couldn't complete the *M'itta lensahn* anyway, without *L'inar* to follow on his body. With a hard thrust of his finger, he penetrated her and the worry flew from her mind. He sucked hard as he fucked her with first one, then two long fingers, and she felt the orgasm he'd begun earlier rush back to engulf her.

Her inner muscles rippled over his fingers, and he licked her juices, prolonging her pulses of pleasure. Before she could recover, he flipped her over, propping her up on her knees before him. He ran a hand over the curve of her ass, squeezing first one cheek and then the other. He traced her *L'inar* there, as well. Unlike some Inarrii women, she had several stray lines curling over her ass cheeks to trail down to her sex from behind. Few Inarrii men thought to stroke them, and David's touch delighted her and teased her with its primal focus.

He bent to touch his lips to her nerve lines, sucking at them gently. She groaned, her body talking for her as she parted her thighs and rocked her hips, asking him to touch her again. Her nipples rubbed against the sheets, teasing them while he slid his finger back inside the lips of her *sinaa*. She shouted out in pleasure.

"Right now, Alinna, you are mine. Let me take care of you."

Said mentally, it was so close to a mating promise Alinna almost stopped him, but she needed this, wanted him. He was so unlike any Inarrii she'd been with, and he drove her desire beyond the level of anything she'd ever felt. Maybe that was the situation, maybe it was the man, but she didn't want to stop.

"Yes."

Her simple answer was enough. He stroked her again and she groaned at the pleasure and the emotion flowing from him—his satisfaction and desire a combination that blasted ay thought from her mind. Gripping her hips, he centered his cock against her sex, then rocked her back against him until he was deep inside her. He groaned, his control clearly on the edge. With a slow motion, he pushed her forward again until his cock sprang free from her *sinaa*. He pressed the wet tip against her again and again, each time penetrating her deeply from behind.

Alinna shivered and swallowed hard. No Inarrii preferred this position. It wasn't formally taboo, but it made her feel vulnerable, something another Inarrii would stop immediately. She relaxed, concentrating on the pleasure, and moaned aloud as his cock breached her yet again. He continued to pleasure her *sinaa*, rubbing the tiny center of her nerve clusters as he thrust slowly against her.

Pleasure built, and she cried out, losing herself to it. Everything in the world disappeared except for the feeling of his hands and cock. David growled her name, his thrusts less controlled. He was nearing his orgasm. The thought of him spilling his seed inside her in this way drove her wild. She bucked back against him. It was enough to push her into a shuddering mountain of an orgasm. Her reaction drove his, and he gripped her hips hard as he pumped his orgasm into her. After a moment, they sank down on the bed. He pulled his cock free of her, its length still hard. He wrapped his arms around her.

"If I open my eyes for real now, will you disappear?" he whispered into her ear, his breath tickling the curve of *L'inar* near her throat.

"Yes."

"Then let's sleep."

Alinna closed her eyes. Her body still hummed with pleasure. How could he imagine sleep would be possible? But she felt his body relaxing behind her. Of course, he thought this was all a fantasy, perhaps even a dream. Slowly she settled against him. Human skin temperature was lower than Inarrii, but it felt good cradled against her back. Perhaps sleep would be possible after all. She felt her eyes drift shut.

Then she groaned as her internal command unit pulsed to life.

"Base to Unit Nine, Alinna Gaerrii, report."

Chapter 6

Alinna eased from the mental rapport that David had established and returned to her body. He would have to sleep without her. She tapped the sensor on the skin below her ear, activating the communications mode of her internal command unit. Although she knew no one from the Inarrii base could see her as she spoke on the focused channel, she sat up in her bed and wrapped her body in the light coverlet.

"Alinna Gaerrii, Unit Nine responding. *Inar tel sahiir.*" She spoke the Inarrii welcome before she could catch herself, then fisted her hands in silent frustration. Using her native tongue on a line that might be monitored was a novice mistake. Being contacted when she had just settled in with David, a Human she'd been meant to watch, had unsettled her nerves more than she'd thought possible. "Is this code secure?"

"We believe it is, although the time until probable discovery is limited." Alinna recognized the deep voice of her commanding officer, Commander Jannii Finar. "Agent

Alinna, are you injured? Do you need retrieval?" Concern laced her commander's inflection.

Alinna swallowed hard against a sudden wave of yearning. She missed her people. Everything was different here, even the scent of the air. At home she could smell the salt of the oceans no matter where she was. Here the hint of chemical air cleaners never left the buildings, and the scent of the forest where she'd landed was so foreign with its pine vegiforms that she would never forget it. She would never get used to the blue skies of Earth either, compared to the warm red mists of her home planet. Only the exquisite pleasure she'd found in David's arms over the last two nights had made the stress she was under bearable.

"I was injured, but I have received medical treatment." Alinna rushed to deliver more information before the commander could assume she'd been discovered. "I'm posing as a Human psychological evaluator. It's too complicated to explain now, but currently I am operating undetected and have gathered more information in the last two days than I have in the last four months."

"That was not in your directive, Agent! We must get you out of there before you are discovered."

"I don't see how that's possible, at least not at this time. I'm located inside Starforce Base One. I am currently conducting interviews under my cover as a psychtech, and I have made a huge discovery—" A sudden rumbling boom interrupted her words. The crystal vid monitor on the wall across from her bed rattled with the vibration.

"What is that?" Commander Finar demanded.

"I don't know…" A second boom sounded, loud enough to echo in her ears.

"Scans indicate the base is under attack. You must leave the base immediately and contact us outside its perimeter."

"I can't. You don't understand, these people are important." Rapid crashes punctuated her words, the final detonation cutting off all communication. An explosion rocked the building and shook the contents of her room hard enough that a glass fell from the bedside table. "Commander Finar?" The coded channel was dead, and she hadn't had the chance to tell her people the most important thing she'd learned: Humans could possess psychic abilities. *M'ittar,* mental communication, was a vital facet of Inarrii life. With it, the Humans had the potential to be true partners to the Inarrii, something they'd found in very few of the other species in the Confederation.

Alinna threw back the coverlet and reached for her clothes as the sound of another explosion resonated through the air. "By the gods, what is happening now?" she muttered aloud. She jammed her legs into the same uniform pants she'd worn earlier and secured the top as she moved toward the exit. Her leg protested briefly with pain, but she ignored it.

Her door wouldn't open. She slammed her shoulder into it, using every ounce of her Inarrii strength. Slowly it yielded, and she was able to force it open enough to escape. Since nothing held the door shut on the other side, she surmised it had been held closed by some security order. Although there was no damage immediately visible, alarm bells sounded in the deserted hallways, and the faint acrid scent of burning plastic tainted the air.

Alinna hesitated for a moment. With the base under attack, this could be her only opportunity to re-establish contact with the Inarrii from her position within the base. If she could access the Human communications line now while the channels were likely filled with defensive chatter, she would be able to use her comlink to hide her messages within theirs. She hesitated, looking left and right down the empty corridors. It was risky. She would have to have direct access through a communications center in order to bypass any active monitoring system. She took a deep, steadying breath. *Passing on the information about the Human ability to use m'ittar is worth nearly any risk.*

Moving into the corridor, she accessed her internal command unit. She retrieved a map of the complex and used the directions it provided to head for the nearest communications command room. Behind her, the crashing sounds of destruction continued, most likely outer walls of the building collapsing under the onslaught of the attack. She shook her head at the folly of navigating through the building. *I'm safer outside. Someone is trying to flatten this place.*

The emptiness of the corridors unsettled her nerves. Alinna opened her senses, trying to make sure that no one had been injured nearby. She had to complete her mission, but these people had helped her. She would do everything she could to help them in return, even if she had to expose herself as she attempted to make contact with her people. Her empathic senses pointed the way. In the direction of the communications center, others had been attempting to flee the building, and several felt either injured or trapped. It was difficult to tell exactly what was happening under the psychic overload of surprise, fear, and anguish.

She rounded the corner of the hall, taking the left turn only to run into a corridor blocked by rubble. She checked the map displayed on her retina, but there was no immediate route to the people on the other side, or to the communications center. Instead she turned around and wound a trail through the hallways, her command unit plotting the pathway as she went. The roaring sound of distant laser fire spurred her on. Her plan was to circle around the hallways until she arrived at an area where she could both contact her people and be of some help to the Humans. Several times, she forced her way through locked doors, slamming her shoulder against them and wrenching their handles past the breaking point.

Finally she reached her destination and started to work her way through the last door. On the other side lay the communications center, and on the other side of that were at least four injured people. The explosions had stopped, but she could still feel the anxiety of the people she was trying to reach. As she breached the room, she instructed her internal command unit to access the abandoned communications computers on the desks all around her. As it attempted to do so, she rushed to the opposite side of the room.

"Hello, can you hear me?" Alinna called. She looked around frantically for something to help her force her way through. In the stark office, there was little to help, and she groaned in frustration as her internal unit told her it was unable to access the Humans' communications system due to the power fluctuations from the attack. She slammed a fist against the metal door, determined to help someone, even if she could not help herself or her cause. The door didn't budge, and she was growing weak. Her leg had begun to throb, the half-healed slash sending waves of pain through her body. Desperately she grabbed a chair and methodically smashed it against the unyielding door.

Alarm bells rang again, screeching in her ear. She threw her weight into the fight but could not get through the frozen access. Her *L'inar* lines stood on edge, and endorphins raced through her system as the stress of the moment ran through her body. She slammed the chair again and again against the door, shutting off her empathic senses against the clamor of Human fear until she got through.

"Dr. MacPherson, stand down!"

Alinna started and turned around to face the person shouting at her. Her breath came in gasps as she realized she'd lost control, forgotten where she was as she struggled to get to those who needed help. A uniformed security officer faced her, his hand resting on the weapon at his side. The blaring alarm had stopped, and the people she had been trying to rescue on the other side of the door were strangely silent. *Dead, or gone?*

"Put down the club, and face the wall."

"Club?" Alinna looked down at the piece of metal in her hand—all that remained of the chair she'd been using against the impenetrable door. Her senses flooded her with the knowledge that the man considered her a threat, and that the people she'd been trying to reach were gone. They'd moved to safer locations and medical help. She shook her head, dropped the metal chair leg and turned to the wall. *How long was I standing here smashing the place to bits?*

Alinna fought for control as she turned her back on the stranger. She shuddered as he touched her wrists. He was binding them together. Warnings from her first days of under-cover training flashed through her mind. This was exactly the sort of thing she was supposed to avoid. She could probably break free, but her cover, or what was left of it, would be blown. *Kahemnit dal,* she swore. Only one thing would make it worse. *Please gods, don't let him see my L'inar.*

DAVID STOOD inside the base security office, where he'd been called to report after the last attacker had been repelled. He resisted the urge to pace the floor. His team hadn't been allowed to join the defense, and the unsatisfied urge to fight, to defend his people, had him on edge. Consciously he knew the team and the new ships were too valuable to launch during a sky-to-base attack like this— they were meant for space maneuvers not air—but damn, it had been hard to sit and wait. These had to be the same people who shot down the airjet—the fact that it had been shot down had finally be retrieved from the flight comp. The protesters had become a serious threat.

Now he was waiting for Alinna, or to find out what was going to happen with her. *What the hell was she doing smashing up a restricted area?* The thought circled around and around in his mind. For the first time, he wondered if Captain Branscombe had been wrong. What if she wasn't a Starforce undercover agent? What if she was with some other agency, one of the anti-space colonization throw-back groups? He clenched and unclenched his fists. *She does have those unusual tattoos...* What if she was involved in the attack on the base? *This is my fault.* He'd known she was there under an assumed identity, and he'd done nothing.

The theory certainly explained her apparent lack of experience when it came to maintaining her assumed identity. An undisciplined rebel group wouldn't provide the kind of training to keep up the façade long term. But it didn't explain how she'd gotten on the secure airjet in the first place, or how she had changed the records stating she was Janet MacPherson. Branscombe swore the methods involved in the record alterations would require the highest level of security clearance. The theory didn't match the need he felt from her either, the sense of loss and helplessness. If she really was from one of the anti-space groups, she'd have nothing but anger and contempt for him. He was career Starforce, a pilot, for God's sake. All he would feel from her would be hatred.

The inner door opened. "Major Brown, please come in." The burly security chief stepped inside and motioned David into the interrogation room. Alinna sat at a table, her hands clasped in front of her, her face serene, but tired. Her hair hung in a ragged mess, and her uniform was in disarray. Her knuckles were scraped and raw, as though she had been in a fight.

David glanced more carefully at Alinna, taking in her slightly sagging shoulders and pale face. Even in her disheveled state, she was beautiful, sensual. If she wore a smile instead of the blank look she now sported, she would appear to have rolled straight from her bed after a night of rough lovemaking.

He grit his teeth. *Get a grip. She could be a traitor.*

"It seems Dr. MacPherson lost her way trying to get out of the building."

David looked at the security officer. The man smiled sympathetically at Alinna. *How the hell did she talk her way out of this?*

"Yes, I tried to make it out of the building, but I just seemed to be going in circles." Alinna spoke quietly, her eyes focused on the table before her.

"The strike is over, the attacking airjet destroyed. Unfortunately, we have no confirmation on their identity." The chief shook his head in frustration. "We've asked Major Brown to escort you back to your rooms. That section received very little direct damage, unlike the rest of the building." He ran a hand over the back of his neck.

"Thank you. I would like to go to my room. I'm quite tired."

David could hardly believe it. The woman had been in a secure area, had a completely flimsy cover story, and they were letting her go without a complaint. From what he'd heard, she'd even done some damage. Surprise turned to annoyance as the security officer offered her a hand to gently help her to her feet. David felt his eyebrows quirk upward and quickly controlled his reaction. *This guy wants her so badly, he's nearly drooling.* David was completely ignored during the exchange, and it did not feel good. His stomach tightened as Alinna smiled at the chief. He suppressed the need to growl at the interaction.

"If Dr. MacPherson is free to go, I'll take her to her room."

Alinna's eyes flicked toward him, the corners of her mouth dropping in a slight frown.

"Of course, she is free to go." The man held Alinna's hand a moment longer than necessary. "But perhaps you might be available later to talk again?" he asked her. "We will need to clear up a few more details."

David ground his teeth together. He watched Alinna smile at the man as she responded to what ought to be a formal inquiry and was instead almost an invitation to dinner.

"Of course, Chief. You know where to find me."

"Let's go," David growled. *Before I knock someone flat. She's got a lot of explaining to do.*

Surprise flickered over Alinna's face. David frowned, wondering if his voice had sounded as abrupt and angry to her as it did to him. She walked to the door and looked with uncertainty back over her shoulder at him. David stalked forward and brushed past her out of the interrogation room and security office. He kept silent as he led her back to the section of the building housing her office and private rooms. If he said anything now, he'd lose his temper, not a great idea with the chief watching them.

"Major Brown," Alinna began, but he marched on,

quickening his pace through the corridors until they reached her room. He paused, staring at the warped and dented door. It was the only damaged thing in the area. The thing had been beaten open from the inside. He glanced at Alinna. She, too, stared at the damaged doorway. Her skin paled further. Only her bright green eyes showed some life.

She took a step forward and swayed on her feet.

"What's wrong?" He grabbed her arm as she swayed further, catching her as her knees buckled.

"Nothing. I just need to sit down, please."

She didn't look at him as he held her with one arm and forced the warped door open with his other. He guided her into the room and kicked the door shut behind him. *No matter what she's trying to pull now, I am getting the truth out of her before I leave this room.* He let go of her arm, and she dropped into a nearby chair with a quiet sigh.

"I'm sorry, I don't feel well. I feel a bit dizzy," she muttered, her lips pressed thin as though she didn't want to admit the weakness to him.

"When did you eat last?"

"Well, I was so busy running the tests this afternoon I missed lunch. And dinner…didn't look appealing."

David shook his head in disbelief. "I don't think you've had much to eat other than those nutrition bars since you got here, have you?"

"No, I guess not. I had a headache at first, after the crash, and then I was busy…" Her voice trailed off.

David grimaced. He closed his eyes for a moment and prayed for patience.

"Wait here." He strode out of the room and across the hall to her office. Touching the compad outside of her door, he tried for a connection to the mess hall. The line crackled from the electrical damage from the attack, but he was able to call for a quick delivery. Then he returned to Alinna's room. She hadn't moved. "I've ordered a supper for you. While we wait for it, you can tell me what the hell is going on." He didn't miss the mild frown of distaste flicker across her lips. "Don't make faces at me. And don't tell me you were lost. You were in a secure ops room for a reason. This time, you're going to tell me everything."

She waved a hand tiredly. "It's not that. You know I can't."

He dragged a chair over to face her. "I don't know anything. Why don't you enlighten me. Who are you?"

———

ALINNA BIT HER LIP. David *did* deserve to know what was happening. His people would hopefully be partners with the Inarrii. She felt more strongly about that each time she interacted with this species, one so similar to her own. David was a good man, one who thought of her wellbeing even when he clearly suspected she had ulterior motives. But she'd sworn to serve her people, and her orders were specific—do not reveal herself to the Humans. The decision to reveal herself and her people's observation of the Humans was out of her hands.

"I can't tell you that."

"Did you have something to do with the attack? Are you with one of the anti-space factions? Did they attack us to stop the new colonization mission?"

"No!" Alinna stood and paced the length of the room, then turned and faced him from the opposite side. She drew a shaky breath. "I had nothing to do with that. That's not why I am here. I have no idea who attacked you, and I have no idea what their intentions are."

"Then why are you here? Who are you?"

Alinna looked at him. He sat there watching her, concern in his eyes and emotion flowing from his soul. He really was concerned, even though suspicion laced his emotions as thickly as desire. It was too much. He wanted her, cared about what was wrong with her. He cared about his team, his people. If his skin were different, he could be Inarrii. Blindly she reached for anything to support her. The stress was too much, and she was too weak. Her leg was burning now. Had she disrupted too many of her *L'inar?* Was there an infection? And her decision to avoid the Human food had clearly been a bad one.

Before her knees could buckle again, he was there. He supported her, pulled her close. She laid a hand on his chest, resting for a moment against his strong body. *If only I could stay like this...*

A chime at the door interrupted her thoughts, intruded on her moment of near surrender. David stepped away to answer the door. Without his support, the pressure of the stress she was under crushed against her. The demands of her duty, stranded here away from any Inarrii relief, overwhelmed her. She had no training to combat this level of constant stress. How much more could she take before she broke and failed her mission completely? She would bring dishonor to her family, her clan...

"Sit down. Eat something, for fuck's sake," David growled at her. She blinked. He'd already answered the door, collected the food, and set it on her small table. Her stomach grumbled, reminding her how long it had been since she had eaten a decent meal. Wryly she wondered if this food would be any different from the horrible gruel she'd been offered in the medlab. She certainly hoped so.

Alinna sat at the table across from David. He watched her as she surveyed the strange food before her. She licked her lips. At least it smelled better than the medlab offerings. The question was, what was it and how did she eat it? She glanced at David, who continued to watch her. "Aren't you having any?"

"Nah, I already ate. You dig in. It's my favorite, since I didn't know yours."

She raised her eyebrows at him.

"Roast beef on whole wheat, with mayo and mustard, lettuce, tomato." He picked up a small speckled wedge from her plate. "Spicy pita chips." He popped the chip into his mouth.

She picked up a chip as well and sampled it. The strange taste tickled her tongue, but she found it palatable. With a sigh of relief, she dug into the meal. This was one stress she could at least relieve. Her body needed fuel, and she couldn't think properly without it. Food would make the remainder of her mission at least possible, if not pleasurable.

"Be honest about one thing. Are you a Starforce Intelligence agent?"

Alinna almost choked on the bite of food. She struggled to swallow, and he pressed a drink in her hand. She drew in a gulp of liquid and choked again as the fiery taste slid down her throat. Finally she gasped for air.

"I am not here to hurt anyone, David. My mission will help everyone. That's really all I can say." She took another gulp of the drink, deciding she liked its bite after all.

"That doesn't answer my question." He watched her steadily sip at her drink for a minute. "I need to know what is going on. Surely you understand that."

Alinna finished the bottle of liquid and picked up another chip. *They really are delicious.*

"I know they are. I love the way they taste with the chipotle spices," David casually replied aloud to her thought. He narrowed his eyes at her. "You did just say they were delicious, didn't you?"

"I did. Can I have another drink?" Alinna hedged. He passed her another bottle, and she immediately took another sip as he watched her carefully. *My shields must be slipping. What is wrong with me?*

"What shields?"

Alinna took another huge gulp of her drink. *Oh, shit!*

Chapter 7

David watched as Alinna guzzled her second beer like an old pro. The drinks were a Canadian brew he'd discovered last year that packed a lot of alcohol with a sharp bite. Alinna wasn't about to tell him everything he needed to know, at least not voluntarily, but from the glazed look in her eyes, the alcohol might give him an advantage. He'd ordered four bottles and didn't intend to drink a single one. He wasn't leaving the room until he had some answers.

"This is really good." Alinna spoke slowly, clearly enunciating her words. Whether it was because of the drink or because she was stalling for time, David wasn't certain. If it was the alcohol, it was hitting her hard and fast. Not surprising perhaps, since she hadn't eaten much in two days.

"I think so. What shields, Alinna?"

She stood abruptly, her drink still grasped in her hand. She avoided his eyes. "Shields? I don't know what you're talking about." She took another gulp of the brew. "Of course I don't know anything about mind shields." Alinna set the second empty bottle on the table next to her half-finished sandwich.

"Of course not." David eyed her slightly unsteady gait as she moved nervously across the room. "Would you like another drink?" *One more ought to do it. The lady isn't used to drinking. And finding out about mind shields sounds like a good place to start.*

"Sure. You bet. Another drink sounds like a great idea." Alinna stood beside him as he cracked the seal on the last bottle on the tray. Since he was off duty, four drinks were allowed, so he'd ordered his full allotment. She reached for it eagerly.

Alinna continued to be a puzzle. She wasn't familiar with the most common things—the security passes, the food, beer—and her looks were beautiful and unusual. But her apparent amateur clandestine behavior, that was the most intriguing mystery. He watched her long neck as she took a deep swallow. A curl of her tattoo peeked through her light brown hair. He took back his musings. The most fascinating puzzle might be if her tattoos really extended all the way to one very hot pussy. His mouth grew dry as he watched her bend over to reach the bottle cap that had rolled to the floor.

When Alinna straightened she caught him studying her. A slow smile broke out over her face. "You're watching me."

"Yes." David drew in a husky breath. This wasn't quite what he'd thought about when he encouraged her to drink that last brew, but he couldn't help responding when her smile grew sly.

She slowly licked her lips.

Damn. He stood, wanting to look her in the eyes.

She stepped closer to him. "I've been watching you,

too." A small giggle escaped her lips, and she brought her hand to her mouth, surprised at her reaction.

David caught her fingers in his. She stilled. For a moment neither moved. *Fuck it. I'm doing this.* David leaned in and caught her lips with his. He kissed her, gently tasted her. The spicy flavor of pita chips and the yeast of the beer didn't completely hide the purely female taste of her lips. When he was about to withdraw, she moaned into his mouth. Desire quickened within him. His cock throbbed into a thick pulsing erection. He drew her to him until they clasped in an embrace. He deepened the kiss, devouring her as he'd wanted to since the moment he'd seen those emerald eyes of hers.

Alinna pulled away from his lips, but only enough to whisper his name. He could feel the heat radiating from her skin, could swear he could smell her desire even in their fully clothed state. But the scent of alcohol laced her breath.

"I want you, Alinna," he groaned and let go of her. *I can't do this. She's half-drunk, not just tipsy.* "But I don't think you are in the right state of mind to make any conscious—"

"I want you, *Ya'lenali.* Don't tell me what I can decide. Don't push me away. I *need* this." Alinna pulled her uniform shirt up over her head, exposing her toned body.

Holy fuck. The tats curve right over her breasts, just like in my dream. David swallowed hard. He wanted to touch her, to trace those fascinating lines over every sweet curve of her body. He jammed his fingers into his hair in frustration. "Sweetheart, I can't do this. Tomorrow, you'd be sorry and I'd feel—"

"You'd feel damn good. Just like I want to feel right now." She stroked her fingers over her tattoos, seductively following the very pathway he wanted to trace, until she reached behind her back and unsnapped the simple bra from her body. When her taut nipples sprang into view, David groaned aloud. "See," she murmured, "they do go everywhere."

"Oh God."

"The gods don't mind. It can be just like the other times only so much better. Want to see where else they go?" She fingered the lines on her stomach, slipped a finger into her waistband.

David growled in his throat. She was toying with him, and damn if he didn't like it. He stepped toward her, and she took a step backward, leading him toward her private bedroom. He couldn't stop himself, couldn't take his eyes off her roaming fingers or hard nipples. He took another step, and another, toward her.

"David, love me like you did last night, *Ya'lenali.*"

David stopped. The thought hit him like a dash of cold water. *Last night? Last night was a dream. Not even a dream—a fantasy.*

Alinna stopped too and reached for him, drawing him into an embrace and a kiss even as his mind raced. She ran her fingers down his back to cup his ass and squeezed. "A fantasy that we could make real, right now," she breathed into his ear.

David caught her hands and looked into her eyes. *Something is really, really wrong here.*

"No it isn't, *Ya'lenali.* For the first time since I got here, something is right."

David shook his head, clenching his teeth in frustration. Alinna's eyes weren't quite focused. She was too drunk to know what the hell she was doing or saying. It was his own fault—that had been the plan after all. But what the hell was she saying? "You can hear what I'm thinking? What I want?"

"Oh, yes, David. I can hear you wanting me, feel it, feel the desire. I want you too."

"Who are you?" He let go of her.

"Just Alinna, a woman who needs you. Please, David." Her eyes filled with tears, and she licked her swollen lips. "Please fuck me."

It was the ragged tone of her breath, and the way her chest hitched on a sobbing breath. David's will was undone. She wanted him, and he wanted her, no matter who she was, what she was. He slid his fingers into the waistband of her pants and slipped them down past her hips, dragging her thin underwear with them. He groaned aloud, dropped to his knees in front of her. *Those damn tattoos* do *go everywhere.*

He pressed his lips to her naked mons and rubbed his skin against hers. Her citrus and musk scent, so familiar, tightened his erection. He ignored the conundrum of her familiarity when he had never really touched her, pretended he hadn't noticed her using an endearment that he'd heard only in his dreams. Instead he concentrated on the incredible sounds she made as she held tight to him. Her body quivered, strained to open her legs, but they were constrained by the pants that had only dropped as far as her knees. Her shudders focused David's attention on her reaction to the binding. Quickly he flipped her onto her bed and pulled the pants the rest of the way down her legs. Alinna gasped, and he checked her expression. A rejection now would drive him insane. But the glint in her eyes revealed her excitement as clearly as her hard nipples and wet pussy.

He pictured her bound to the bed, a vision that left his mouth dry. Better yet, he imagined her long legs splayed open and held up by bindings suspended from the ceiling. It was a fantasy he'd had before but never indulged. With access like that, he could lick her until she begged for mercy.

"Please, David," she begged, echoing his dream. She writhed on the bed before him, her need almost desperate. He knelt on the floor beside the edge of the bed. She lifted her hips to him in a show of unabashed lust. The action brought a grin to his face. He'd satisfy her, but he'd get some answers out of her, as well. He traced his fingers over the curling tattoo on her left thigh. The color of henna, but definitely permanent, the edge of the artwork was clean and sharp as if she'd just had the ink placed on her recently. His attentions brought a moan to her lips. "Please, you can…tie me…if you want."

He stilled. "You can see what I am imagining. How is that possible?"

"Don't stop. I can feel your emotions, your desire, and when we touch, I can hear what you are projecting."

He stroked the curve of her tattoo again, this time a little closer to her inner thigh. She had his complete attention, both sexually and intellectually. He ran his fingers over both of her legs and inhaled her aroused scent. She wriggled, tried to lift her hips in response, but he held her down. *Control. Keep it in control.*

"Why do you have to be in control?" she gasped as he traced the lines pointing directly to her clit.

"Because you need so badly to give it up. You need to trust me. Tell me the truth."

"I am telling you the truth."

"How did you learn to read minds?"

"I don't." She reached down to touch herself, and he caught her by the wrist. Pushing her arms upward, he rose from his knees to climb up onto the bed to press against her until her arms were above her head and he was centered against her hips. Her skin radiated a heat and a citrus scent that had him panting with the desire to lick her again. With a free hand, he stroked the marks on one breast until he reached her nipple. He rolled it between the pad of his thumb and his finger, tweaking it until she cried out.

"You don't read my mind?"

"No," she panted, "I read your emotions. Sometimes your thoughts just shout out at me, but you do that, not me. I feel what you feel until you make the connection. Then I can hear your thoughts." Her words slurred slightly and she fought to pronounce each one with exaggerated care.

"And how did you learn to do that?"

"I was born with it."

David rocked his hips against hers. He could feel the heat of her right through his military-issue pants. This was as much torture for him as it appeared to be for her. He wanted her so badly, he could taste it. He tried a different tack.

"Where did you get these tattoos?"

"I was born with them, too. David, please!" She hooked her legs over his back, struggled to rock harder against him.

He ground against her wet heat. *Fuck, I can't take this much longer.* He'd never had such a responsive woman. She reacted to every touch, every caress. Sweat beaded on his forehead. Then it dawned on him what she had said.

"Born with them? Born with these tattoos?"

"They aren't tattoos." Her eyes were glazed as she groaned out the words. His hips continued to rock a rhythm against her that he couldn't seem to control. "They're *L'inar.* Sensory nerve lines. The more you touch them the more I want you, *need* you." She kissed his neck, licking and nibbling as she went. It was getting harder and harder for him to think, to ask the questions he needed to ask. More than anything, he wished he could simply make his uniform melt away, as he had in his fantasy, so he could drive his throbbing cock home into her hot pussy. She was so wet, she was drenching his pants. Or was that his wetness seeping out? He shook his head.

"What the hell are you talking abou—"

Alinna cut off his words by stealing his breath, pressing her lips to his and drawing his tongue into the hot well of her mouth. She tasted like sin, so hot and so good. His body screamed at him, "to hell with asking anything else." He wanted her too much to give a damn about what she was saying, although her readiness to accept his fantasy of domination still had him reeling. *Control it, man!* He pulled back and stifled a groan at the action. She clung to him, moaning as she licked at the sensitive skin on his neck.

Abruptly he stood, ignoring her protests as he let go of her and moved away from her heat. He ripped his uniform shirt off and threw it to the floor, then yanked his undershirt off, as well. Fingering the soft material, he took a deep breath. *Control.* Moving quickly, he rolled the cotton undershirt into a cord and began to tie it over Alinna's eyes.

"What...stop!" She struggled, turning her head away and raising her hands to push against his chest.

"Trust me."

She hesitated. Her eyes were already covered, but David could see the tension in her body as she debated his request. Finally, after a moment, she lowered her hands.

Hot triumph flashed through his veins. She was his, would do as he asked. She didn't trust him yet, not fully, but by giving him the power here in bed, the rest would follow. He finished tying the makeshift blindfold over her eyes, the bright white cotton looking starkly primitive against the golden hue of her skin and the light brown of her hair.

She shivered in his hands. His cock throbbed in response, insisting upon being released from the tight confines of his pants. Quickly he stood and yanked off his shoes and the last of his uniform. His cock jutted in front of him, and he stroked it standing over her. Gritting his teeth, he resisted the insistent urge to bury himself to the hilt in her sweet pussy. Her lips parted as she waited, probably wondering what the hell he was doing.

Without thinking about what he was doing, David grabbed her discarded uniform and tied first one of her legs and then the other to the bed frame. He ignored her tiny mews of shock and snatched up her shirt to tie her hands together above her head to the headboard. He stood back to admire his handiwork. Splayed on the bed sheets, she had to be the most luscious woman he'd ever seen. He grit his teeth. Control might be more difficult than he'd thought as he stared at the curving marks covering her from elbows to knees.

"David…" She whispered his name as though she was afraid of what he was going to do next, but her hips rocked on the bed, slowly, her uncontrolled motions causing whispers of sound as her binds rubbed against the sheets. His heart pounded at the sound—he had no idea what he was going to do either, but with his mission at stake, there was no way he was leaving this bed without answers, no matter how hard he might have to push her.

Chapter 8

Alinna's heart raced. She'd never felt so sexually aware as she did at this moment. As an Inarrii, she was well-versed in sex and the many pleasures it could provide, but with David, the level of surprise over his methods and her reaction to them continued to mount. She'd never been asked to give away control like this. In a race that continually used the direct mind touch of *m'ittar*, everything was shared, nothing experienced alone. But with her abilities concentrated on the empathic side of *m'ittar* and with David's untrained gift, she wasn't sure what would happen next. She trusted him, trusted him to at the very least please them both. To not know what he might do or how he might do it was exciting, and a little frightening.

A tingle of fear crept through her *L'inar*. She felt the nerve lines shivering, stiffening. She didn't fear for her life or her body, but the excitement she felt was so different it was triggering her instinctive response. For once, she welcomed the reaction and enjoyed it as it zipped through her body. She gasped aloud in pleasure and imagined what she might look like to David as she heard his matching intake of breath.

"What the fuck?" His voice reflected the emotion he was projecting to her empathic senses—shock, confusion.

Alinna shivered. Thank the gods that the lust remained underneath the rest of his immediate reactions.

"I told you, they aren't tattoos."

"What…" The touch of his cool skin against her *L'inar* had her moaning aloud. Under his hands, they dropped flat again, the reaction slow as fear and excitement remained high in her emotions. But his touch was sending conflicting messages of passion straight to her *sinaa*. If she could have spread her legs any farther or reached to touch herself, she would have. She bit her lip, trying to remain still as he touched the lines again.

"What are you, Alinna?"

"I…I am Inarrii. I am from a race far from this system."

He stopped, pulling his hands back. His emotions blanked—he'd slammed down that barrier again, one she had no idea how he'd learned to create. Her heart sank. She yearned for him. By the gods, her body *burned* for him. If he rejected her now, she wouldn't be able to bear the stress or, she realized, the loss of his company. When had she come to care so much? It didn't matter. She needed him, now.

"David, please. I am still a woman. Don't leave me like this." Her words met silence, and she strained against her bonds. The soft cotton over her eyes felt like a prison, and she felt her *L'inar* begin to stiffen again as panic set in. Urgency forced her to do something she had never done before; she projected her emotions on him, threw the power of her fear and desperation and longing at his psyche. When she felt his hand reach out to touch her thigh in a comforting grip, she sagged in relief and passed that on to him too, her relief, her lust, even the loneliness she'd felt since arriving on this foreign land.

"Shh." He comforted her without promising anything. "That's how we were together before. You touched me with your mind." He idly stroked her *L'inar*, smoothing them flat against her skin. Pleasure and joy hummed through her nerve lines, and she sent that emotion to David, as well. She strained against the bindings, desperate to touch him, to be touched. The waiting, this was something that no Inarrii would do to another, make them wait for a response or even to ask for it.

"*M'ittar*—the gods' greatest gift to us. To you apparently, as well. Your thoughts brought me into your dreams, David. I couldn't get there by myself. I can only sense and send emotion on my own. I need contact from another mind to have a true exchange of thoughts and experiences." Her tongue slid over the Human words in desperation. Thoughts seemed harder to form, although whether it was from his strange foods or being controlled sexually she wasn't sure.

"You're beautiful." His casual caress hesitated. "But how much of all this is bullshit? What the hell are you doing on Earth?"

"Don't stop," she murmured. "I swear I'll tell you everything, but don't stop touching me. I...need you." She cleared her throat. A wave of confusion hit her. She tingled, everywhere, and it was becoming more and more difficult to concentrate when all she wanted was for David to take her, to use her and please her and never stop. Never would she have imagined trying to explain her race while she was tied, naked, to an alien bed. "Inarrii need sex to maintain our calm, to remove stress. And I have been *very* stressed since I got here. Our dreams together have barely kept me going."

He remained silent. Alinna's anxiety grew. The glimpse David had given her of his darker fantasies had been frightening, but exciting. He wanted to control her body, and she was handing him complete control, both of her body and her future by revealing her true identity and nature to him. She pulled against the bonds on her wrists, reminding him silently that she was at his mercy. She suspected she could use her strength to free herself, but it would be difficult, and would mean the end of any bond of trust she and David might have begun. If they took this further some day, she knew he would discover her limits and probably push her beyond them. There would be no way of escape. Excitement slid through her at the thought. A part of her that she never knew existed hoped he'd get the chance.

"What *are* you doing here?"

"My shuttle crashed. It was brought down by the airjet that crashed on your base. I was disoriented and injured. When I regained consciousness, you'd already labeled me as Dr. Janet MacPherson. Since I couldn't get back to my ship and couldn't reveal who I was, I made sure the comps here agreed with that idea."

"You look like us." He put both hands on her thighs, and she shivered in delight. His desire radiated from him like heat, so warm she could almost feel it on her lips.

"Except for the *L'inar.* They're really nerve lines. They react to fear, excitement and…" she gasped as he stroked the lines on her lower abdomen, "and pleasure."

"And to pain?"

"Yes…" She stiffened as a sudden image crossed the mental barrier he'd erected. She saw herself bent over

David's lap as he slapped his bare hand across her ass. "Are you going to torture me after all?"

"Perhaps."

Alinna squirmed on the bed at the sudden intensity and promise in his voice. Her movements seemed to focus his desire, she could feel it on her as the block between their minds slid away and *m'ittar* deepened between them.

"ARE you hearing what I am thinking?" David pushed the thought at Alinna. Her nakedness, and the way she shuddered under his hands, made it damn hard to concentrate on the craziness unfolding around him. His cock hadn't flagged even when she'd proven without a doubt she wasn't Human. The way her skin stiffened into ridges along the marks of her tattoos—her *L'inar*—it was weird, but not unattractive. The ridges were narrow and not very tall. They felt like the crisp edge of a neatly pressed seam against the satin of her skin, and every curving ridge raised in a fascinating design under his fingertips along an erotic pathway to her very wet pussy.

Considering the way she responded whenever he gave these new erogenous zones the merest touch, sex with her would always be exciting. More than that, his own secret fantasies were fluttering wildly through his mind. She'd hesitated, but she was clearly excited both at being controlled by him and by being rewarded for her surrender. He'd never had a chance to experience this level of dominance. In the military there were many levels of authority and control, but control was not allowed to become sexual. Sex between peers was allowed, but even implying a desire for sexual dominance with a female at any level within the force could end his career, and he'd been in the forces since he was eighteen.

The irony wasn't lost to David. He'd found his ultimate bed partner, a sensual woman who responded to his every touch, who welcomed his darker fantasies, and she'd turned out to be an alien who might be a spy sent to end the Starforce entirely, not just his career within it. The choice was his for the moment, to keep her or report her, but the truth would come out eventually. And what then? What was she really here for? Whatever it was, he wouldn't be the one to discover her true intentions. The moment anyone knew of her true nature, she'd be snatched from his grasp and given to the You-fos—finally justifying the division within Starforce Intelligence Department dedicated to the discovery of alien life forms.

He had only a few hours with Alinna. Then he would have to report her. *Hell, I should report her now.* But the thought left him empty. She lay still on the bed before him as he contemplated the problems her reality presented. The citrus and musk scent of her skin wasn't from any sort of perfume. It was a part of her, an erotic foreign element rendering her as desirable as any Human woman he'd ever known. Held as she was with his makeshift bindings she was even more desirable. He barely knew her, barely understood what she was, and had no idea what she was really here for, but he couldn't let her go. Not yet. She was everything he'd ever wanted—even down to his career. He'd lived his whole life with dreams of space. His curiosity burned nearly as brightly as his lust. Alinna could tell him a lifetime's worth of stories about a life on another world, and she could bring his fantasies, both the light and the dark, to life.

"I hear you, David."

He closed his eyes as her mental voice touched him.

Like his dream, he could feel her mentally caress him, her fingers trailing lightly along his arm as she spoke. He opened his eyes, preferring the reality of her bound body laid out like a feast before him, one he shouldn't indulge in.

"I understand that you have to report me, David. I knew it might come to this, but believe me, I am not here to hurt anyone. I trusted you, let you bind me. Trust me, and mate with me in the flesh, just once. Let us both have something for now."

Her thoughts mirrored his. David nodded, though he knew she couldn't see him. The affirmation was for himself as much as an agreement to her thoughts. There'd been enough thinking. He wasn't about to let her go.

Instead of answering her, he ran his fingers over her *L'inar.* She rocked her hips in response, her lips parting. She let out a sigh of what he thought might be relief. He stroked her along her right inner thigh, then along her neck. He touched her slowly, feeling the heat from her skin, the temperature much hotter than his own as he caressed her soft curves and flowing lines. He kept moving, changing the places he touched so she wouldn't know what was coming next. Her sighs became moans, growing more and more excited.

Unable to resist, he touched her with his tongue, tasted her taut nipples and hot skin. He licked at the beautiful *L'inar* designs, working his way down to her pussy. She thrashed beneath him.

"David, let me touch you, please!"

"No." He slapped lightly at her thigh, punishing her for demanding. The feeling of being in control, of pleasing her at *his* pace, was making him crazy. The real question wasn't whether he could control her, but whether he could control himself. He watched her *L'inar* ripple from the place he'd slapped. Her breath hitched, and he glanced up at her face to judge her reaction. The way she licked her lips and moaned removed any guilt he might have felt about punishing her.

"Trust me, do as I say, and I will give you everything you need."

She licked her lips again. Her mouth invited him. He leaned in to kiss her, and she arched her back to thrust her nipples up against him.

"Naughty." He moved up the bed, slowly taking the time to drag his skin and his cock up the length of her body to kneel with one knee on either side of her stomach. He leaned in, dragging his fingers over the *L'inar* running up the inside of her arms to her elbows. Carefully he pushed his hips forward until his cock centered over her mouth. Without asking, she parted her lips, but hesitated to take him in. Satisfaction poured through David. Already she was learning to wait for his cue. He stroked her *L'inar* in reward.

"Lick me," he commanded.

The hot breath of her moan purred over his sensitive skin. He gritted his teeth and prayed for strength as her tongue darted out to touch the side of his cock. After a moment she seemed to gain her confidence. She tasted him, savored him as she licked in circles around the base of his cock. She pressed her face into him, reaching past the curls of hair to suck at first his thighs and then his balls.

It was too much. With a groan of frustration, David pushed his fingers into her hair, held her still while he parted her lips with his wide cock and watched them stretch to take him. He pushed in slowly, wondering how much she could take, but her eager sucking pushed aside his concern. He shuddered as he lost control for just a moment and thrust hard into her willing mouth.

ALINNA SUCKED hard at her mate, willing him to come in her mouth. If he'd had *L'inar*, she would have followed at least the most important ones for the ritual, those encasing his *saiin* and the skin around his Human testes. He'd already followed her lines with his tongue, beginning the mating, and made his promises, even if he did it unknowingly. If he came in her mouth now, the normal end to the ritual, they would be mated.

If he were Inarrii, of course.

She nearly cried in frustration when he pulled out of her mouth.

"Naughty. I will come when I want to, sweetness. You'll have to be punished for that."

Alinna felt her body flush. "Punish? But I didn't do anything!"

"You know you did. And now for complaining about it, as well."

Alinna stiffened. He was *laughing* at her. She'd almost mated the alien, and he was laughing at her. Worse, she realized as he lifted himself away from her and lay down on the bed beside her, worse was that she *wanted* it.

She shivered. *What is wrong with me? I've been too long away from the Inarrii. I...want...him to do something.* Everything the Human did in bed was mildly shocking and incredibly pleasurable. Even his position above her as she sucked him —an Inarrii male would have lain on his back while she licked at him, giving her the freedom to do as she wished. David took what he wanted, but he gave back everything and more.

Alinna gasped as David laid his hand flat against her *sinaa*, his big palm covering her. No sooner had she thought about how good his touch felt than he gave her wet skin a light slap. Shock and pleasure radiated from the tiny *L'inar* curling over the most sensitive skin on her body. She jerked, tried to clench her thighs shut as the pleasure took her almost to orgasm.

He slid a finger inside her, and she groaned his name. Slowly he withdrew, dragging wetness with him. He reached up and pinched her nipples before she could protest. The mild pain competed with the embarrassment she felt over her reaction and the sensation pulsing from her *sinaa*. Without warning, he repeated the slap to her wet skin. This time she did cry out, uncaring for the moment that he knew how much she liked his punishments. Ecstasy raced though her *L'inar*, and when he slid his finger inside her again, the pulsing sensations pushed her into the beginning of orgasm. Greedily her inner muscles clenched at his invading finger.

"No, no, sweetness. Not yet." David pulled from her and moved off the bed.

Alinna groaned in frustration. Obeying might kill her after all. When she realized he'd left the room, she began to worry. A noise in the outer room told her he hadn't left her quarters. Her heart beat hard. He wouldn't report her already, leave her unsatisfied and give her away? She was about to call out when pressure on the bed, and his cool touch along the *L'inar* of her thigh, reassured her he wasn't gone yet. But unsettled fear remained in her stomach.

Alinna jumped when David ran his fingers over her *sinaa*. His emotions were calm, focused and filled with lust. Fear was again forgotten. She moaned as he pushed open her inner lips, but the shock of something hard and cold being pressed against her was too much.

"Stop! What are you doing?"

David ignored her struggles as he stroked her sensitive skin. Alinna wiggled, realizing the freezing cold came from a piece of rapidly melting ice. Cold water dripped against her. She struggled against the ties on her wrists, but found they had tightened against her. She'd been right; he was testing her limits.

"Please, David. That's cold!"

"Let me make it better." His hot tongue licked the tight bundle of nerves at the core of her *sinaa*. Immediately the denied orgasm quivered to life within her, only to be put off again as he pushed another piece of ice against her.

"David, I need to release!" She pulled once more against the binding. "You keep stopping it."

"I know."

She whimpered. Immediately he withdrew the ice and licked her again. Pleasure rocked through her but was quickly eclipsed by the intense sensation of his cock, now feeling as hot as any Inarrii as it thrust against her, pushing her *sinaa* wide open until she took him all. His weight settled on her hips as he took her, driving his cock deep.

"Ya'sai lenali..." She called out to him until he covered her mouth with his, the hot smoky taste of his tongue mating with hers as he pumped his cock deep inside her. The words continued to resonate in her heart. With them, she admitted again what her body had been telling her— she loved this strange man. As her body began its final surrender, the shuddering waves of ecstasy rocking through her, doubt was pushed aside. She'd take him to the stars and show him her world.

Chapter 9

I ntense pleasure rocketed through David as he thrust within Alinna. She shuddered and called his name as her orgasm shattered through her, her pleasure and joy resonating within their shared mind contact. She'd called it *m'ittar*, but he'd call it heaven as his body reacted and his balls tightened. Muscles corded and strained with ecstasy as he seated himself deep within her. With a roar, he came apart, his seed shooting deep inside her.

For that one moment, he was complete.

Alinna pressed her face into his neck, murmuring words she'd said before. Her fluid language reminded him of the vids he'd once heard of a Polynesian singer. The auditory reminder of her foreign background made him raise his head to stare at her.

What the hell did I do?

He should have reported her the instant he knew something was off. But he hadn't. He'd let her continue her charade as a psychtech, and when he'd discovered she was something far more alarming than an internal spy, he should have marched her right back into the security office. *Fuck. I screwed an alien, as well as my career.*

David rested his forehead against Alinna's. She took the opportunity to leverage her lips against his, her kiss gentle. He should have turned her in, but he hadn't, and the worst thing about it was he was glad he hadn't.

Reaching up, he snagged the ties around her wrists, pulling at the knot until she was free. He stroked the soft, straight locks of her hair and slid the blindfold up over her forehead. She didn't say a word, simply wrapped her arms around him, hugging him and looking at him with those bright green eyes.

Peace. David let himself relax. He listened to Alinna breathing underneath him and briefly thought about rolling off her. Instead he remained still, not wanting the moment to end. If he moved, things would change, and the peace would stop. He didn't want that to happen, didn't want to be forced to make a decision that would eventually end what he'd found with Alinna.

It was more than sex, although he could never tell her, and he hoped she would never find the truth within his mind. He felt something for her. Felt more than a desire to possess her or take her. He felt a connection, and it scared him. If he admitted it, what would he have to offer her? There could be nothing long term between them. He had his career, or at least he hoped he still did when this was over.

But more than a career, the Starforce was a home for him. Alinna must have a career too, and he had a suspicion that he would not like what it was.

"Alinna..." David began, but was interrupted by the insistent chime of his compad. The unit was still attached to his pants, now lying crumpled on the floor.

"Shit. What now?" he growled as the compad blurted

an urgency level reading he couldn't ignore. He took a long breath, savoring the sharp citrus musk scent of Alinna's heated skin. Then with a single fluid movement, he rolled away. She opened her arms, released him as he moved, her fingers trailing along his arm as he parted from her.

Grabbing the compad, he barked out an acknowledgement. "Yes."

"Major—," panting breaths nearly eclipsed Branscombe's voice, "—they're here!"

"What? Who's here?" David caught Alinna's attention, placed his finger against his lips in a motion for silence, then shook his head. *"Don't say anything."* He threw the thought at her, and she nodded. *"There's definitely something to be said about this way of talking."* He thought he saw an answering spark of amusement in her eyes, but was certain of it when she responded.

"If we were talking— you were shouting."

"…Starforce Intelligence Agency! They're shutting it all down!" David tuned back in to what Branscombe was gasping into his ear.

"Say that again?"

"The You-fos are at the lab, and it's only a matter of time until they head your way. They want to talk to you, and to *Dr. MacPherson.*"

David's blood ran cold. Alinna's eyes widened as she stared at him. *Fuck.*

He cut the channel. "Get up, quickly." He bent to untie Alinna's ankles. The scent of sex curled around him as he moved. "There are people on their way here who are looking for you."

"David, I have to get out of here. I can't be discovered. It will ruin everything."

He stood and grabbed for his underwear and uniform pants. "I don't know why you *are* here, Alinna, but I sure as hell don't want to be found like this."

"You mean you don't want to be found with an alien. With an alien you had sex with," she corrected herself, moving a little slower than he to reach for her clothes, but reaching for them nonetheless.

"No, I really don't, but not because I am ashamed of being with you." He grabbed her arm. "I can still feel what you're feeling, Alinna." He stared at her, but her emerald eyes avoided his as she muffled the mental contact between them. "I don't know exactly what they are looking for, but I don't think it's going to take them long to put two and two together—not when they are already looking in the right direction. We have to get you out of here."

"You might not want to have anything to do with helping me when you know why I am here," she murmured.

David zipped up his pants and made a grab for the undershirt he'd used to blindfold her with. She'd pulled on her cotton underpants as well and was yanking up her pants as she spoke. Her motions exposed the curving *L'inar* along her back. *Beautiful.*

"Okay, why are you here?"

"You know everything else, so you might as well know this. I was stationed here, well on the dark side of your moon, to observe your base and learn about you."

For a moment his heart stuttered. "To invade?"

"No!" Warmth and reassurance rushed back to him. He felt the emotion as though a gentle hand pressed against his chest. "Never, David. I am Inarrii. We are an honorable race. We are here to find out if you would be a good match—if you could be a partner in the Confedera-cy." She did touch him now, her hand catching his, her eyes looking deep into his. "We are here to offer a Treaty."

David felt a chill run down his spine. *Warm fuzzy feelings or no, no one offers something for nothing.* "What do you want from us?"

"You have resources, minerals, people. We have technology and can offer you protection."

"Protection from what?"

"The Raveners—a group of thieving, murderous races —roam space looking for unprotected planets. They take what they want and destroy what's left. If they haven't found you yet, they soon will. We did. The Intergalactic Confederacy is strong and large enough that our presence here, even if we are only negotiating a Treaty, will prevent them from attacking your world."

David moved again, his thoughts whirling around him. Perhaps it was cynical, but he had a hard time believing anyone could be as truly generous as Alinna made her people out to be. He yanked the undershirt over his head. It smelled like her. *Damn.* He grabbed his uniform shirt, pulled it on over the undershirt and worked hard at keeping his thoughts and emotions calm. He'd just taken this woman, used her to fulfill a fantasy that had been in his mind for years, and if he had the chance, he'd do it again. He wanted to spend as much time as he could with her. *But not at the expense of my world, my people.*

ALINNA SHOOK HER HEAD. David was blocking her. Somehow he had learned to keep her from reading her emotions. She dressed quickly, but she watched him from the corner of her eye. He moved stiffly, abruptly. Perhaps he thought that by hiding his emotions, he could lie to her, but his body told the truth. Despite the trust she'd shown him and the fact that she'd told him the truth about her mission, he didn't believe her. Or at very least, he was uncertain of her motivation.

There wasn't time to convince him, but without his help, she doubted she could get back to her ship, to her people. Without his help, the Treaty might be over before it started. It had happened before, distrust driving entire races away from the Confederacy and right into the arms of the Raveners. She rushed to finish dressing. There had to be a way to convince him and find the emotions she'd sensed beginning to blossom within his heart. There had been caring there, and hope.

She was shoving her feet into the soft-soled shoes of her uniform when he surprised her again.

"You must have learned a lot running those tests on my team."

She glanced at him. His face was stony, his movements tight as he strapped on his heavier boots. "I did."

"What did you expect to learn from me?"

"What I learned from them. That you are an intelligent, caring, funny, compassionate and passionate people. Complex, but generally honorable." She took a step toward him, but he turned away.

"We have to get out of here, right now." The terse words rang with the same tension she could feel within him.

"Where are we going to go?"

He glanced back at her. "Damn good question. Come on."

David stalked to the door. She followed, then dashed back to the room to grab the emergency pack hidden away in one of the bedside drawers. When she turned back to follow him again, she nearly crashed into his wide chest. He'd come back when she didn't follow immediately, and now he gripped her arms. His face could have been part of a statue carved from stone and dedicated to the gods, except for the narrowness of his lips and the angry tick of motion along his jawline.

He snatched the bag from her hands, struggled with the opening until he ripped the *tocuh* seal on the pouch. She let him rip at it. He needed to take his anger out on something. He stared at the contents.

"Emergency rations from home," she said, "or the wrappers from them anyway. I wasn't sure how to get rid of them."

"The recycler would have done it."

"I couldn't get the thing to open up."

Amusement glinted from his eyes, and Alinna felt relief flash through her like a flood over the wash plains of her home. She swallowed hard. What he thought, what he *felt*, meant so much to her. The relief seeped away at the thought. She'd given her heart away and doubted she would get it back. She closed her eyes against the result of her own stupidity, only to find herself jerked along by her arm as David dragged her with him toward the door.

"Your ship crashed. That's what we found in the woods. You melted it, how?"

"Internal self-destruct mechanism. Why?" She couldn't follow him, not his thoughts or, it seemed, his pace. She stumbled as he paused to wrench the door open and scan the corridor.

"It was pretty small. You couldn't have been coming from very far."

"I didn't." She debated within herself. *You've told him everything else; tell him everything.* She couldn't do that, not quite. She couldn't tell him she loved him, or that they had nearly completed the Inarrii mating ritual. "That was my observation pod. My shuttle is on your moon, dark side."

"Come on." He grabbed her hand and dragged her into the hallway with him.

"Where?"

David stayed silent, moving them along at a brisk pace and checking the hallways as they moved.

"There's no one in the next hall if we are going to stay on this route," she told him. Her leg began to ache again as she kept to his pace.

"You can sense that."

It wasn't a question, but she answered him anyway. "Yes, and you could too, if you were trained."

"Trained. You're looking for pets?" The grip he had on her elbow tightened.

Alinna broke her stride, coming to a complete stop. According to her internal comlink, they were nearing the security office, but also the exterior wall of the building. David needed to make up his mind now. Turn her in, or help her escape.

She wrenched her hand from his.

"Trained the way I am, to read and understand emotions and thoughts, to share them with another. *M'ittar* is a celebrated gift and is shared with my people and yours. That, more than anything I have learned about your people, is worth crashing on your planet. But if you are going to be so paranoid that you're going to drag me to your security office and tell the world an alien has been spying on Starforce, that I used some sort of power to make you sleep with me or whatever else you are worried about in that blocked-up mind of yours, then go ahead."

David stared at her. Then he blinked and shook his head, a grin breaking out over his wide mouth. "Are you done?"

"Are you?"

"Nope, but we'll have to get out of here before I can

talk to you anymore about this." He grabbed her hand again. She let him, finding a seed of joy within herself that pushed her to keep pace with him again. She had no idea what he found funny about her or this situation, but a twinkle of humor glinted along the edge of his mental barrier.

They passed the corridor that led toward security and turned left instead. Alinna's internal map told her they were about to leave the building. Was he hiding her in the woods? She couldn't stay there for long. Worry had the *L'inar* along her shoulders tightening. "David..." Her voice trailed off. She blinked in the sudden stream of bright sunlight as he threw open the door.

"Just stay calm and follow my lead." He gave her hand a little squeeze.

DAVID CUT across the field outside Building 4B. A dusty trail broke the short-cropped grass, and he followed it, taking the same pathway he and his pilots had used for the last several months while on the base. The first time they'd walked this way, Second Lieutenant Sven Olens had lain right down on the green stalks and rolled. David sighed. What he was about to do went against everything he and his team fought for. He was about to kill any chance he had left of being a team leader, maybe of even being a pilot. He was about to risk his future, perhaps his life, and maybe even the safety of the world.

But he believed her.

He felt it—knew it in his bones. She was telling the truth about who she was, what her people were, why they were here. And he hadn't missed the fear in her eyes or her voice when she talked about the Raveners. Whatever they were, they were a threat to Alinna's people and to Earth.

Maybe he had been brainwashed. Maybe he was doing exactly as she had planned, rescuing a damsel in distress— a spy, for God's sake. Or maybe he was just thinking with his cock. Maybe he'd just take her back to wherever the hell she came from and just go home, pretend this never happened. Sweat dripped down the back of his neck inside his uniform. That would never happen. Whatever fucked-up thing he was getting into, it would never be the same again.

He should go back. Even now, he should stop and drag Alinna back to security. *Nope, not going to happen.* Whatever arguments his head might come up with, his gut knew better, and this far into his life as a pilot, he trusted his gut.

"Major Brown." A young patrolman came to alert and made his salute as David and Alinna reached the shuttle hangar.

"Sergeant." David prayed that Alinna was right behind him, her senses or powers or whatever she'd used on security before ready for use now, should they need it.

The patrolman stepped aside, allowing David and Alinna to pass through the small gate into the building. The large hangar doors were closed, probably still in reaction to the recent attack. The building had twelve-foot-thick walls of plasmetal comp alloy and was about as close to laser-proof as possible.

David walked steadily to the flight unit room, grabbed up a suit and a helmet, and motioned Alinna to do the same. She frowned when she looked at the helmet, but her face cleared when he plopped his on his head. She did the same and silently worked her legs into the flight suit. He signed the gear out on the local comlink, noting he was taking his ship out for a practice run, and signed

Alinna in as Lieutenant Angie Lee. With his ident registered, she didn't need to enter hers, since he was only registering one ship out for an in-atmosphere practice run.

He yanked his flight suit on and watched Alinna struggle with the set he'd thrown her. It would have been funny if this wasn't the most stupid thing he'd ever done in his career. Finally he worked the zippers and snaps for her, sealing her into the suit. It was for her safety, but it didn't hurt to feel her under his hands again. His mouth went dry, and not just from the fear of losing his job. He could smell her. He wanted to bury his nose in her hair, to kiss her again, to make love to her. Instead he slapped her helmet visor shut.

"Major Brown, you aren't scheduled to make another practice run until fourteen hundred, sir."

David grinned when he turned to the admin at the door. "Little change of plans, Eddie. Things have been happening so fast around here, we've got to blow off a little steam." Eddie dreamed of flying but it would never happen. Even modern science couldn't make the man see again after he'd lost his vision to a chemical flare. Eddie understood the need to fly, though.

"Gotcha there, Major. I'll amend the flight plans for you." Eddie had already turned to the comlink before he'd finished speaking. David motioned Alinna ahead of him, and they walked out the door as Eddie was still inputting the change.

David linked his com to Alinna's helmet com and opted for sub-vocal, setting the security levels on the compad to level nine, and individually pass-coding the lock. "We need to get on a ship now before they look for us and discover the flight plan change. You sure of your ship's location?"

"You sure you want to help me this way? Perhaps we could find someone in your government who would listen."

David kept moving toward the main hangar, picking up his pace as he considered her words. "No, we need to get you out of here. There are people here now who have been looking for aliens a long time, and I don't think they're going to be too happy to find a spy or believe your Treaty is real."

"But you do. You believe?"

"I'm getting you out, aren't I?"

David swiped his ident over the hangar door and walked into the main shed. Massive overhead lights shed a bright glow over everything. Black metal glinted along the surface of the fastest space fighters ever made by Human hands. David's heart thumped hard, pride flooding him. Eddie must have done the job as the flight path lights were kicking up, and the drones pulled out his ship, lining it up for him. He took a deep breath as pride turned to pain. This might be the last time he got to fly as anything more than a passenger, and that would be as a prisoner when Starforce realized what he'd done.

The ship came to a stop. He strode forward, wondering what Alinna thought of the beauty, but then decided he was glad he didn't know. Glad she was quiet as they climbed the steps to the dock and walked up the ramp into the ship. He ran his gloved hand over the doorway for luck, for comfort.

"Major Brown to flight admin, we are on board." He took his seat, saw Alinna sit out of the corner of his eye in the co-pilot chair. He strapped in and waited until she had done the same. He caught a glimpse of her face through her visor. Her eyes were worried, her lips turned down in a frown. Had she learned that watching Humans—learned their facial expressions, or were her own naturally similar?

He turned back to the controls and laid his head back into the headrest. The security monitor for the ship lowered its monitor to his face, a lens distending to make identification through the patterns inside his eyes.

"Pilot identity confirmed."

The hangar doors slid open, and David began his standard sweep of the controls. Droids pulled the ship to the gate. David nodded when the vid alerted him he was ready, but he knew it already, felt the wheels leave the ground and fold into the smooth underside of the ship as he hovered three feet above the ground on the droid leash. Some people couldn't feel the difference, but he always had.

"Hang on," he sub-vocalized to Alinna. "This is the fun part."

Chapter 10

The ship soared into the sky like an agile bird. David handled the craft with skill, with style. Alinna imagined the muscles cording in his arms inside his flight suit as he gripped the controls. His abilities, his confidence in the sky, reminded her of the control and the strength he'd shown her in bed. The thought sent shivers of sensation along her *L'inar*.

"I need the position of your ship."

Alinna brought herself back to the mission at hand. She fired off the coordinates, but David looked at her blankly.

"That's great," he muttered. "Can I have the location in Starforce coordinates?"

Alinna swallowed. She sensed he felt angry—little waves of fury sloshed over his barriers and against her. *He's sorry he helped me.*

She reached out to tap a control pad. Once again, her time studying the Earth language proved invaluable. "These are the coordinates of your base, and these are the ones for your new Mars base. If we use them as reference points, the comp can understand my directions."

"I can take it from there."

"I'm certain you can." Alinna hesitated, and then reached out her hand to touch his arm. She needed contact with him, even if it had to be through her gloves and his heavy suit. If they made it to her ship, he would likely abandon her there. But she should be grateful he would do that much for her after her deception. He would leave her there and return to his home. He avoided her eyes, keeping his fixed on the starscape.

She sighed, pulling her hand away from him and settling it on her lap, and looked out at the fast approaching moon. Regret flooded Alinna. Her lies, even while necessary to the future of both their people, ensured that David would never desire a formal mating, would never complete the *M'itta lensahn* with her. She took a deep breath. She couldn't expect or even hope for anything better. No, she would concentrate on the hope for a new Treaty. The Inarrii had never found a true partner, even within many species of the Confederacy. Humans could be what the Inarrii had hoped for when they joined the intergalactic gathering of races. Life would be interesting. It would be good, she told herself, even if it had to be alone. The honor she would bring her clan would push her career forward rapidly, and her family would benefit in so many ways. Not that those benefits would make up for his absence.

David brought his ship down low over the surface of the moon, skimming the pockmarked surface close enough that she could see the walls of the shallow craters. The man was born to fly.

"You're very good."

"What?" He glanced over at her.

She cleared her throat. "You're very good at flying."

He pressed his lips together and looked away. "We're almost there."

Alinna swallowed. He was shutting her out. "I need to deactivate the shields, or we could fly right over it and never know it was there."

"Really? You can't even see it?"

Curiosity was far better than anger. "You can't see it. Your ship can't detect it with any of your scans." Alinna activated her internal comp, sending out a signal for her ship to lower its shields. She grimaced. Dropping the shields would send a signal back to the secret Inarrii Jupiter Moon base. It wouldn't be long before she either received communication, or a visitor. David would be gone before that.

"What?"

She hadn't realized David was still watching her. She summoned the strength to form a small smile. "Nothing. There it is."

"She's a beauty."

Alinna glanced at her ship, nearly a third larger than the fighter David commanded. Snub-nosed, but tapering out in a sleek elongated oval, her ship was a welcome sight. At least she would be comfortable there when David left her.

"Dock on the left side. Just set down beside the ship, and it will hook us up, create a sealed dock."

David's eyes narrowed as he contemplated the landing. He held the ship in his control, bringing it smoothly down in a controlled descent. His landing was probably better than she could manage, and she'd been flying since she was a junior. With a gentle bump, the two ships locked together. *Inarrii and Human—a good match.* She held back a sigh.

Hopefully the Treaty would be more successful than her brief Inarrii-Human alliance.

"I understand you have to go back now…" she began.

"Hell no." David released his seat's magnetic grapple and pushed himself away from the command seat of his ship. "I'm not going anywhere. I showed you mine, now you show me yours." He waved in the general direction of her ship.

HE SHOULD GO. But the flip words about checking out the alien technology flew from his lips, and he knew he meant them. He wanted to see an alien ship up close and personal. It might be his only chance. And damn it, he didn't want to go. If he left now, he had nothing to return to other than the abrupt end of his career. There was no way he'd get away with dropping her off here and just sliding back into his life.

He ground his teeth together. If he left now, he'd have to say goodbye to Alinna. There'd be no chance of ever seeing her again. He ached to touch her, hold her, make love to her. *Fuck*. Even after he discovered her lies. Even when he had to consider the question of how truthful she'd really been about even the sexual side of their relationship. Had it all been lies? Spy stuff? Convenience? Maybe.

It was the maybe that was killing him.

He really couldn't believe it. Not completely, and therein lay the rub. Her desires meshed too perfectly to his. What were the chances?

Alinna led him into her ship. Her bouncing gait and casual grab of the convenient handholds was the same as any long-term spacer in the weightless environment of space. No small ship used gravity control, the energy drain judged too high for the minor convenience. As he followed her, he could feel her, although he was doing his best to pretend to himself he couldn't. How he had come to be able to sense and experience her emotions was beyond him. It had to be her. He'd never sensed anyone else's emotions like this. Sure, being aware of his team's emotional status made him a better commander, but it hadn't been the same.

He'd already had her. He should be able to let her go, this woman from a strange land, a strange people. She'd needed him, so he'd helped her and satisfied them both in the process. He'd fulfilled a fantasy he never imagined could come true, at least not without paying a sexu-temp a huge amount of money. Paying to dominate someone was pretty much a contradiction of terms. It didn't mean anything. What he had shared with Alinna…if she had been Human, it might have meant everything. The fact that she wasn't Human…hell, it made it even better.

David tore his eyes off Alinna, forced himself to pay attention to her ship. This was another fantasy. An alien technology. Who among the Starforce pilots didn't imagine meeting an alien? Didn't imagine a first contact, a major discovery? He'd dreamed of this since he was a child. Not that there was anything to see in there. The walls were black, featureless as they moved into her ship's dock.

Alinna slapped her palm against a flat pad in the final docking lock. The hatch slid shut behind them. She pulled her helmet off and motioned for him to do the same.

"This is it."

"What? Everything is…flat. There's no controls."

"Hmm? Oh." She slid a finger over the pad. In seconds, the walls, the floor, the ceiling, every surface glowed to life with tiny luminous patches. Ever changing, the flow of lights seemed to form pictures, words perhaps, and then flit away as he stared. "Sorry, one thing we don't share is quite the same visual range. That should help you to see. Put your hand here." She motioned to the flat pad.

David laid his hand where hers had been a moment before. The panel warmed under his skin, and he felt tiny patterns rising to his touch. The heat and texture reminded him of Alinna's *L'inar,* and he snatched his hand back, disturbed.

"The ship will recognize you now as an ally."

"We haven't signed your Treaty yet. Hell, no one even knows you're here but me."

"True, but they will. After I make my report, my people will be in contact with Earth, probably within hours of verifying what I've seen."

"You'll tell them what you saw of the base? Of my ship?" David's heart pounded. *She's seen our defensive capabilities up close and personal after the attack on the base.*

"David, they know all about your base. What they don't know is about you." She shook her head at him and turned away. The hatch slid open, and she pushed away from him, using the low gravity to propel herself forward. He followed her, one hand gripping his shed helmet and the other grasping handholds along the wall as he moved.

"About the mind-talking thing."

"Yes." She turned a corner and floated into a wide room.

David hesitated. Clearly this room encompassed her private living quarters. The walls and ceiling reflected a hologram of a deep red sky, cloudless and vibrant compared to the shadowed tones of the black flooring. Her bed, a wide platform against the back wall, seemed out of place. Part of him wondered how she managed to rest against a mattress without gravity to hold her there. Another part of his mind wondered if the images of the red sky were from her home or someplace she'd visited. He couldn't acknowledge the tiny voice inside of him that asked what it would be like to make love under the red sky as they floated weightless.

"They need to know about your ability to achieve *m'it-tar*, but they also need to know you are compassionate. Thoughtful, honest, honorable."

She'd begun to pull off her flight suit. The air inside her vessel felt warm against his face, and he wondered how much power went into keeping the place from freezing while she hadn't even occupied the craft for the last week. The Inarrii had technology that surpassed his. She'd been telling the truth about that. *Hell, she's telling the truth about everything.* Relief seeped into him, warmed him. He'd made the right decision for humanity after all, even if part of it had been dictated by his cock. Now he just needed to find out if he'd made the right decision for himself.

"I doubt my commander is going to find me so honest. I expect they want to kill me right about now." David pushed off from the handhold on the back wall to float toward the other end of the room. Through an open hatch, he observed what had to be her cockpit. It wasn't so different from his. He glanced back at Alinna. She was struggling to remove her leg from the last of the flight suit clasps. Bent at the waist to reach the tab, her sweet ass looked heart-shaped. She wasn't so different from a Human either. But her *L'inar* caught his eye, reminded him of her intense response to his touch.

She was unlike any woman he'd ever been with. She didn't feel ashamed to lose herself in sex, didn't think it made her less in his eyes or more. She was comfortable with the part of her that needed him. It felt damn good to *be* needed. That much about their relationship was different.

Alinna shook off the last tenuous grip of the flight suit, the action sending her weightless body up toward the ceiling. With a rolling flip, she corrected her path and used the impetus to move toward him. Her sweet lips turned down slightly at the corners.

"I feel responsible for the trouble you will face when you return." She caught a handgrip and hovered near him. He could touch her, if he just reached out with his hand. "But you have to know that the Confederacy will offer your people a Treaty that could save your entire world." She reached out for him, touched the skin on his cheek with her fingertips. "Because of you, the Inarrii will ensure that the Treaty is more favorable than you could imagine."

"Because you can hear my thoughts? What if no one else can do it? What if I'm just…different?"

"If one Human can attain *m'ittar*, then many will likely have the gift. I'm simply lucky to have met you and be able to prove the gift exists." She leaned in, touched her lips to his. "I'm lucky to have been with you."

He deepened her kiss, tasted the desire in her.

"Open yourself to me, David. I want to share something with you."

"We don't have time, sweetness."

"Not that." Humor twinkled in her eyes at his remark, but her mouth held a serious line. "Open your mind."

David hesitated. He *did* believe her. Did believe in what she said her people were here for. But doing as she asked, it wasn't just a matter of listening to her. It was allowing her to touch his soul. If there was any way she could hurt him, this was it. Never mind losing his career—that was likely gone now. Opening to her meant he could lose his heart.

Fuck, he thought. *Might as well face it—you already love her, or you wouldn't be here, no matter how good she was in bed.*

"I'm here."

Alinna looked into his eyes. He shuddered, then stilled as he saw what she wanted him to see: her memories, her home. Her people. Men and women in some sort of short skirt-pants, their chests bared to the air, played on an ocean shore unlike any he'd ever imagined. Black sand and red skies competed for his attention in the vivid landscape, and the scent of salt permeated the air. A beautiful woman with long brown hair laughed and sang a song with a simple melody to an audience of captivated males, their hair even longer than hers, and their *L'inar* flared in pulsing ridges as they listened to her song.

"Is this what your life is like?"

"Yes, these are my people. My mother. My father was killed by the Raveners as he fought to protect another planet."

David saw it. He saw the grief, the pain that crowded Alinna's life when her father died. Felt her passion as she moved upward within the Inarrii forces. Understood her disgust and feeling of impotence as she explored a world already ruined by the pirates. The very pirates who would likely find and decimate Earth.

"Alinna." He reached to touch her and realized he still wore his flight suit gloves. "Damn it." He dropped his helmet and ripped his gloves off, rushed to touch her again. "I can't stay."

"I know."

"But I want to." He stroked the soft skin of her neck, followed the line of her *L'inar* in a gentle caress. "Don't think it is because I don't want to."

David opened his mind to her again. It hurt to show her his past, but he offered her what he could. The memory of his parents finally admitting they were severing their marriage felt as raw and painful now, showing it to her, as it had when he was little and so alone. Alinna

117

responded with a pulse of warmth, and he sighed with relief. He'd been lonely for a long time.

She leaned into his hand. A shiver ran through her shoulders. He let go of his handhold to wrap his arm around her, burying his fingers into her silky brown hair. He held her, melting into her embrace as though they were one. He sought her lips, took them, took her and kissed her with the passion burning inside him. This could be their last moment together. Whether he had a future to offer her or not, he ached for more time together. After what he'd just experienced though, he had to make sure that his people were ready, that they understood the threat and the necessity of the Confederacy's offer of a Treaty.

He had to leave, go back and explain it all, now.

"Base to Major Brown, we request confirmation of your location."

The compad in his helmet blared Eddie's request. Alinna stilled in his arms, and he sensed a quiet withdrawal from her as though she waited to see how he would respond. For a moment, he did nothing. Alinna's jade eyes watched him. Finally he sighed and released her, pushing away from the wall to grab at his free-floating helmet.

"Major Brown here. I am making a swing of the moon, Base One. Is there a problem?"

"There are several officers here looking to have a chat with you and your guest."

Eddie didn't sound too happy. The implication that he was aware, as were others, that David had lied about who had boarded the ship with him was easy to read. David ground his teeth together. There would be no time to make love to Alinna again. No time to explain to her what she was coming to mean to him.

"We will be completing our swing of the moon in twelve minutes."

"Base requests visual confirmation, Major."

Sweat trickled down the inside of David's flight suit. He licked his lips and thanked God he'd locked the controls on his compad and on the ship. It would take hours for the base to force control over either. "We are on the dark half of the swing, Base One. We have had a slight malfunction, and all visual is out at this time."

"Base One requests full compliance, Major. Return to base immediately."

"Copy, Base One, ETA in…fourteen minutes." David flicked the channel shut. "Fuck, fuck, fuck."

"They'll be waiting for us."

"If we go back now, you're done, the Treaty is done." David slammed his fist against his thigh. "Damn it!"

"You believe me, then?"

He pushed off the floor and floated to her, pulled her to him. "I believe." He drew her in for another kiss. "There isn't time for this, though. We need to get you out of here. They'll be watching this area." He gestured toward the cockpit. "This doesn't seem like a long-range ship, unless your technology is a hell of a lot different than ours. Do you have a base nearby?"

"Yes. But if I move the ship, they'll probably be able to pick me up, now that they know there's something to look for."

David ran a hand through the short spikes of his hair, tugging them in frustration. "Okay. Where is your base?"

"Jupiter, the largest moon. What are you thinking?"

"If they see your ship, they'll be on you before we clear the moon's gravity. The You-fos are waiting for it, I'm sure. If we go in my ship, we can be halfway there before they realize we aren't coming back."

She gripped his arms, her fingers pressing deep into the

thick fabric of his flight suit. "You can't. You won't just lose your career. You'll be arrested."

"Sweetheart, I don't think there's much chance I'm going to get anything different. I'm in this, Alinna, all the way. Just make the Treaty worth it, okay?"

Chapter 11

David shut off all communications as he fired up his ship for the trip to the Inarrii hidden base. Guilt ate at him, but not as urgently as the need to protect both Alinna *and* his world. If he could get her to her people, one job was complete and the other well begun.

"We've got a ten-minute window before they realize we aren't returning to Starforce."

"That won't get us to Jupiter. The base is on the fourth moon, the one you call Europa."

"By the time they realize we're headed somewhere else, it will be too late to catch us."

Alinna fell silent. When he looked at her, her visor faced the navigation vid, its angle too steep for David to see her face. He pressed his lips together, clenched the controls a little tighter. No doubt she felt the tension within him. *Hell, if I had any more stress, she'd likely smell it, even through her helmet filter.*

There was no going back, only forward. He watched the Inarrii craft complete its disengagement of the docking hatch. The moment it completed the cycle, he pushed his ship into a steep ascent, driving it just beyond the recommended acceleration level for de-orbiting. Levering the controls, he set the course manually, disengaging the auto-nav in case Starforce opted to attempt a remote control of the ship when they realized he'd gone AWOL. He kept to the dark side of the moon, using it for as long as possible to shield his direction from detection. They wouldn't be expecting him to head away from Earth. Even if he were trying to escape and take Alinna somewhere, where could they expect him to go? The abandoned moon base? The unfinished Mars encampment? Not likely, not enough places to hide.

He checked the ship's energy level. Even at the exhaustive pace he'd set, there was more than enough power to reach Europa a dozen times over. Eddie ran a tight division —David didn't doubt the man had personally ensured every ship in the squadron was completely battle-ready, even though their mission wasn't set for another month.

So much for that mission. David's thoughts turned grim. Everything would change when the Inarrii approached the Human council about a Treaty. It would make the conflicts over the Mars settlement sound like a squabble over a child's game. Earth would either come together for a while, or erupt in chaos. Until, of course, they understood what the alternative was. The Raveners could mean the end of the world. That, beyond anything else, must be stopped.

David added another degree of speed to the set course.

"I'm going to contact my commander and let him know we're arriving." Alinna's terse words and abrupt tone had alarm bells sounding in David's mind.

"What's wrong?"

Alinna hit the control to release the magnetic force holding her in her seat. She floated upward, pushed against the seat back to move into the main body of the fighter.

David turned his chair to face her, but made no move to release his seat restraints. If anything were to go wrong he wanted to be within easy reach of the controls.

Unlike Alinna's craft, his fighter ship had only the cockpit and a cramped living quarter, barely more than a pair of tethered bunks, a food re-heater and a recycler as well as a tiny lavatory. He watched Alinna float around, apparently absorbed in checking out the restrictive space.

"Alinna."

"When we get there, you'll have to leave again, right away. Starforce will know you're up to something, that I'm missing, but they won't have to know that you were... aware...of a spy and didn't report it. You could say that I changed my mind about going up with you. Eddie didn't actually see us board."

"It's gone too far now. You must know that. How could I explain your absence anyway? They know or at least suspect I've decided to join forces with you."

She pulled her helmet off. Procedure required that occupants of a ship keep all flight gear on at all times while the ship was in thrust mode, but David couldn't blame her. The sight of her chestnut hair floating loosely around her as she moved—exposing her *L'inar*—had his cock tightening in his flight suit.

"I wish we had taken my ship. We would have had more room...we could have taken a few minutes to ourselves," she grumbled.

"I'd want more than a few minutes."

She looked up at the heat in his voice but then looked away. "I...I guess we won't be getting them."

"What would you have done if we had the time?" David closed his eyes, taking in the sound of her voice.

"I would have touched you like this."

David felt her hands running over the back of his neck,

running down the curve of his pectorals. His eyes flashed open, but she hadn't moved. He shut his eyelids again, a smile creeping across his lips.

"This mind stuff is great. You would have touched me…"

"I would have touched all of you." Soft caresses roamed his body. His cock throbbed, pulsing and growing with every beat of his heart as her touch grew more erotic. When her lips found the tip of his erection, he groaned out loud.

"I'd have wanted to touch you too, sweetness."

"I know, but I want this. I want you in my mouth, Ya'lenali."

"What does that mean?" He struggled with the thought. Her lips, imaginary though they were, made concentration nearly impossible as she kissed the length of him, then worked back to the tip to take him deep inside her mouth. She sucked hard and then soft, her tongue caressing, milking him. He sank his fingers into her hair, rubbing the tips against the *L'inar* he knew were there. She moaned in response, and the sound broke his resolve. He bucked up, fucking her mouth until he came, spurting inside her greedy lips.

"It means 'my love.'"

David pulled her close to him, held her against him. In their shared mental contact, they were skin on skin, and heart to heart. *"I love you, Alinna."*

A soft tone chimed.

David blinked his eyes open to find Alinna had floated close enough to touch him. Her green eyes reflected the black space in the viewer beyond his shoulder, but he didn't need to look back. The chime meant they had passed the window of time that their motions would go undetected. They were now seven minutes from their destination. A second alert blurted. They were being hailed, but their closed communications channel would not respond.

"We're almost there."

Alinna moved back to her chair, pulling herself closer until she could initiate the magnetic grappler. She tapped the skin behind her ear. "*Tel sho ahoi.* This is Agent Alinna Gaerrii, Unit Nine. I am approaching Inarrii Jupiter Moon Base in a Human vessel. I am accompanied by Major David Brown."

"*Inar tel sahiir,* Agent. You are expected. Base out."

David raised his eyebrows at Alinna, silently asking how they knew. Alinna smiled. "They would have been monitoring my ship. They greeted us with honor. They'll be glad to meet you."

David swallowed hard. The light above the incoming comm channel continued to blink, but he ignored it.

In moments, the shadow of Jupiter became more distinct. The moons loomed, and David pulled back on the acceleration, hauling back on his ships controls until he could approach Europa at a safer speed. Alinna pointed out the security satellite as they passed it, disguised as an orbiting rock. Even prepared, he couldn't stop the gasp that slipped from his lips. The base was far more extensive than he had imagined. Several very permanent-looking buildings, nearly as large as his own Base One set-up, gleamed in the darkness, their surface coming to life just as the walls of Alinna's ship had when she had adjusted them to his optic range.

"Cut your acceleration completely, and they'll bring you in."

David followed Alinna's instruction and felt the ship hang motionless for only a moment before a steady force drew them down toward the base. He sucked in a breath through clenched teeth. Alinna reached out and touched his arm through his flight suit. The guiding power drew them in, past a polarized field, until the ship set slowly down in a huge hangar. Activity bloomed around them,

Inarrii and those David could only describe as androids or…others…moving toward the ship. None wore protective gear, and all appeared to be comfortably grounded—atmosphere and gravity were clearly not a problem.

"Come, there are many here to meet you. These people will treat you well, David. Remember that what you represent is hope for your people and mine."

David released his seat's grapple and moved with her toward the hatch. His heart still raced. *Damn. Here come the aliens. Hope to hell this was a smart thing to do.*

ALINNA FELT the anxiety rolling off David. No wonder he was worried. What had she done but abuse his trust from day one? The Inarrii as a people would do the right thing—offer the Humans full protection with the hopes that they would become the partners the Inarrii were looking for.

As an individual, however, Alinna had done everything wrong. She'd spied, lied, dragged David into her problems when she couldn't handle the stress. That she felt anything for him was a fact that ought to be ignored; she didn't deserve him. In her deluded desire to keep him, she'd even given in to the fantasy of completing *M'itta lensahn* in their mind contact.

He wasn't her mate. She had no rights to him. Because of her, he'd be forced to lose his command. Even when the Humans became aware of the entire situation, understood the threat they faced, it would be doubtful that anyone in the Human military would trust him again. She'd probably grounded a gifted pilot for life.

As the Inarrii and Confederacy contingent on the base gathered to greet David, to thank him for returning her and to have their first contact with a Human, Alinna slipped away. It only took a moment before she was out of his sight, although his confused feelings followed her through the corridors of the moon base. She staggered with grief. *I'll never see him again.*

"Agent Alinna, I would have a word with you." The concerned mind contact of Confederacy Examiner Asler Kiis brought a wave of sorrow over her. The soft touch of his hand on her shoulder finished her. She sagged until he was forced to support her. "Come with me." He led her into an empty side room, helped her take a seat on the low cushioned bench. *"What is wrong?"*

"Nearly everything." Alinna drew in a sharp breath, steadied herself. As an Examiner, Asler Kiis had a reputation for the utmost sincerity and honesty. Perhaps this was just what she needed. She'd intended to speak with someone about David's position, to try and help some way.

"Is it the Human? Have we misinterpreted your report? Do you wish to amend your recommendation?"

"Gods, no. The Humans are more than I have been able to pass on. You will find David to be a compassionate, honest, trustworthy man. He has the gift of m'ittar."

Kiis radiated surprise for just a moment, the bright flash of the emotion like a ray of sunlight through clouds to her empathic senses. He controlled himself quickly.

Alinna continued. *"Examiner…I have violated this man's trust. I would ask that you act on his behalf, make sure that he's given a position on the greeting team and within the powers of the Treaty."*

Asler's bright emerald eyes stared into her own. His expression grew even more serious. *"I have been appointed Advocate on the Human's behalf for any Treaty negotiations, so I could do this. But I believe you'd better explain."*

Alinna ran tired fingers along the edge of her *L'inar.*

The movement was not lost on the Examiner. *"Do you need relief? I can call someone…"*

"No." She spoke aloud. "I don't want anyone." She stood, paced the tiny room. She turned back to him. "I want you to examine my memories, take them for your report to the council. You will find that Major Brown is the kind of man I mentioned." She rushed to get through the next words. "You will also find I have treated him badly. I lied to him."

"As you were forced by your position to do."

"I dragged him into this, and now he'll lose the trust of his people, lose his command and his dream of flying."

"A risk a man of his position would have understood."

"I…took advantage of him sexually. I entered his dreams. I… wished for M'itta lensahn."

Asler's eyebrows quirked upward, but his emotions were so tightly held, she couldn't get a true reading of them.

"You invaded his mind?" His low rumbling voice remained steady despite the horror such an act would imply.

"Not exactly. His untrained *m'ittar* pulled me in—"

"You influenced him then with your skill in empathy."

"No, he made *me* feel, feel things I never would have thought to experience."

"Then what did you do wrong?"

Alinna stared at him. What had she done *wrong?* "I wished for *M'itta lensahn.* He doesn't even know what it means. I wished for something for me, and now he has lost everything."

"Alinna, we all wish for our perfect mate. That's not wrong. Let me read your memories." He held up his hand at her quick intake of breath. Though she had asked for this, most Inarrii disliked the touch of those in the Examiner's office. "Just a light reading, enough to see what happened. I will not make you live through them again. It'll be enough for council."

Alinna bent her head. She owed David everything. Allowing Kiis to review her memories was a small payment. At her unspoken agreement, the Examiner laid a hand on her arm. After a moment, he released her.

"All will be well, Alinna Gaerrii."

———

DAVID PACED the floor of the private room for the hundredth time, it seemed. The place felt less and less like a welcoming area and more like a prison with every moment that passed. Alinna had disappeared in the press of his initial welcome in the flight hangar and now, no matter whom he asked, there was no answer forthcoming about her location. *What the hell did I do wrong? One minute, she's giving me the best head in my life and telling me I'll be welcomed by everyone like some kind of hero and the next, she leaves me in the cold.* His mind ran in circles and he kept coming back to one thing: *I told her I loved her.*

He'd met the representatives from her people, and those in their Confederacy that were able to stand the Earth-style atmosphere, and although he'd found them strange, they seemed as sincerely happy to see him as Alinna had said they'd be. But then a chime had sounded for some sort of event or meeting—he wasn't sure—and they'd all trooped off.

What the hell was happening?

Maybe it was taboo to love an alien. Sex might be acceptable, but love? David ran his hands over the short spikes of his hair. Maybe they were under attack. Who the hell knew what was going on? "Damn it, I want her here now."

"I'm sorry, but we will need to talk first."

David whipped around. A huge hulk of a man in long robes had entered the room silently behind him. *No one that tall should be that quiet.*

"I apologize. I will attempt to make some noise in the future."

David pulled his mind shut, as much as he could. "Stay out."

"I apologize again. Your thought was unshielded, so I assumed you were speaking to me. I am Examiner Kiis, and I have some news and a few questions." He smiled and raised a hand. "Many questions, but only a few that are pertinent at this moment and to your case. First, Agent Alinna Gaerrii fears that because of your involvement with her, your career has been, in effect, destroyed, no matter the outcome of the Treaty."

David pressed his lips tightly together.

"Ah, I see that this is likely correct. She has also asked that you be given a position of honor among the Inarrii and a part in the Treaty so you might get your life back."

David's stomach flipped. The day had more surprises than he could have imagined. "I would be honored," he managed. "But where is Alinna?"

"Are you aware she attempted to make a formal mating with you?"

"What? What does that mean?"

"She wished to mate with you for life. Perhaps it was because you were the only male she could seem to connect with while she was in a stressful situation. Inarrii do not handle long term stress very well." He paused, his eyes focused on David. "Or perhaps it was because she came to care for you during her time on Earth."

David sank onto a nearby bench. For a long moment,

he didn't move. He loved her. And apparently, she loved him. Or the alien equivalent of it if that's what mating even meant.

"Where the fuck is she, then?" He snarled the words.

The big Inarrii's voice remained calm. "There will be some who will claim that such a mating is illegal. However, after examining her, I believe it could be legitimate, depending on your actions now that you understand the meaning."

"The meaning of what, exactly?"

"Her actions—she would have allowed you to touch her a certain way, encouraged it and allowed you to mark her."

"I don't understand." David stood again, resumed his pacing.

"You would have traced her *L'inar*, licked them and deposited your essence in her mouth."

"Yes." David swallowed hard. The memory had him tight by the balls. "We did that...well, sort of. Some of it was during mind contact."

"If you were to do that again in person, and knowing what you were doing, Alinna would be your mate."

David stared blankly at him, this stranger who'd come to explain the facts of life to him, alien-style. "We'd be married?"

Examiner Kiis shook his head. "More permanent than that. She would be yours and you hers, for life."

David blinked. Every couple he'd ever known, including his parents, had been married and divorced a few times over. *She'd be mine.* His mouth ran dry, and a shudder rocked down his back. All his life, he had fought for control. All his adult life, he had desired both to possess and to belong. This was the feeling he'd had from the moment he'd met Alinna.

Some of what he'd been thinking must have passed to Kiis—he nodded and the corners of his stern mouth tilted upward.

"Now you can see her."

The big man stepped to the doorway and touched the command panel. The door slid open, and Alinna stood on the other side. The Examiner nodded to her and walked away without looking back.

David focused on Alinna. She'd only been gone for a few hours, but she looked exhausted. He took a step toward her, and suddenly she was in his arms, kissing him as though she would never stop.

David peeled her Starforce uniform shirt off, taking time to stroke every curve of the winding *L'inar* on her arms and neck. She moaned, leaning in to him, letting him touch her. *Thank God we both ditched the flight suits, or this would take far too long.* The thought had him laughing as he kissed her again.

"You're shouting again." Alinna smiled into his eyes, her mental voice as warm and caressing as her kiss.

"I love you."

She shivered in response but answered slowly. *"If you do this, and Starforce won't let you come back, you'll have to stay here."*

"They'll let me back." He tongued the lines on her throat, following their plunge into the cleavage of her breasts. *"They'll want you. But you're mine."*

She shivered in his arms. "I know you want things."

"I want everything. And you were made to give it, Alinna. You're mine, and I am yours."

"Inar tel sahan yowlenaii."

"What does that mean?" He pulled her bra off, baring her nipples to the air and to his mouth.

"Forever," she gasped.

David flipped her over onto her back on the low couch.

He ripped at the snaps on her pants, not caring if he ruined the closure. "I'm still going to want to tie you up." She moaned, shuddered as his fingers stroked her *L'inar* along her hips. "Still going to spank you when you're naughty."

"Yes, *Ya'lenali!*" she ground out as his tongue licked its way along the same path as his fingers had taken. "Yes!" He ripped the soft cotton of her Starforce-issue underwear until he could see her naked mons beneath.

"Oh," she whimpered as he fingered the wetness between her legs and bent to lick and suck at it. He sucked hard at the cluster of *L'inar* near her core and thrust two fingers deep inside her.

"But most of all, I am going to love you," he whispered, mind to mind. With his words, she came, her waves of pleasure washing over them both in their shared mind.

"I'll take more time with you, sweetness, after we kick some Treaty butt, but first, make me yours." David zipped down his pants, freeing his cock.

She never hesitated. She wrapped her lips around his cock and sucked. There was no finesse, no control, and it had to be the most erotic thing he'd ever felt as she drew him into her, showed him the stars and made him a part of her forever. Their minds joined as his seed spurted into her mouth.

"Inar tel sahan yowlenaii." He stumbled a bit over the phrase, but he showed her what he meant, sliding down to lie beside her and holding her in his arms. *"I will always love you."*

She reached for his hand and placed it against the liquid heat of her pussy. *"And I will always be yours, my mate."*

Afterword

A Note from the Author About The Inarrii Language

One of the things I loved most about the Inarrii was their language. I've spent some time creating a phrasebook so I could remember from story to the next, and found myself interested in their spelling, grammar, and syntax (so sue me, I'm an editor when wearing a different hat and name).

Here are a few from the first book, expect this list to grow:

Kahemnit dal – a casual swear like shit

Tel sho ahoi – sos signal

Tel sho ahoi sho amnetii – sos ship down

Sho Amnetii Gohan yi – ship self destruct.

Sinaa – Inarrii pussy

Tocuh – a type of touch seal

Ya'sai lenali - asking a lover for more – begging for more – asking for more pleasure

Lin'thal – soul

About the Author

Lilly Cain is a wild woman with a deep throaty laugh, plunging necklines and a great lover of all things sensual – perfume, chocolate, silk! She never has to worry about finding a date or keeping a man in line. She keeps her blond hair long and curly, wears beautiful clothes and loves loud music. Lilly lives her private life in the pages of her books.

All of the above is just so much silliness. When not living up to her pen name, Lilly lives in Atlantic Canada, although she spent eight years in Bermuda, enjoying the heat and the pink sands. She returned to her homeland so she could see the changing of the seasons once again.

When not writing she paints, swills coffee and vodka (but not together), and fights her writing pals for chocolate (true story).

Lilly is a single mom who loves reading and writing, dabbling in art and loving and caring for her two daughters. She loves romance in all of its varying heat levels. She loves the chilling moments and the humor in her novels as much as the steaming hot interludes. Her stories are an escape and a release, and she hopes that they can give you that power, too.

To contact Lilly and to find out more about her books, reach out to her website at http://www.lillycain.com

Coming up next? *The Naked Truth - Book 2 in The Confederacy Treaty Series* Releasing in ebook format July 7th, 2020. Check Lilly's website above for dates and links.

Also by Lilly Cain

If the love story in Lilly Cain's *Alien Revealed* swept you away, don't miss her other high heat books! And, catch a sample of book two, *The Naked Truth*, at the end of this book!

No Reservations

No Restraints

Working on Wicked

Return to Me

Building Magic

Dark Harmony

Between Moons

High Stakes

Read a sample of book 2!

Chapter One

"Fuckitall," Captain Susan Branscombe slurred as she woke to the sound of gunfire and running footsteps. She lay on the cold floor of an empty storage room; only the light from the force bindings on her arms and legs provided any illumination. She shivered then groaned in pain as the trembling motion brought cramps to her arms and legs. If they didn't unbind her and let her up soon, she wouldn't be able to walk.

She grimaced in the darkness. Even that tiny motion sent waves of pain across her face and down her neck. She wasn't sure she'd be able to walk anyway after the last beating.

Susan could taste blood in her mouth. The coppery tang would have made her retch if she hadn't strictly controlled herself. She wasn't certain how badly she was injured—one wound on her leg seeped and bled where she'd been burned, and her arm was definitely broken, along with several fingers. Dried blood caked on one cheek pulled as she grimaced, and her head throbbed. *How bad is my face?* They'd cut off her hair and sliced her cheek and nose.

Before she could begin to pity herself, the floor heaved in a sudden explosion.

They were under attack. Not surprising. She'd told them the way to the base and now she would die, along with the terrorists who held her captive. At least she could end it knowing her fellow Starforce Marines would defeat them. They were a kick-ass bunch, every one of them, and she was damn proud to be among them, even if this was how it ended.

Another booming explosion threw her against the wall of the tiny room. *This is it.* Soon the walls of the ship would rip open, and she would die in the cold void of space. *Thank God.* She was so tired of pain; death would be welcome. She waited, but a final explosion didn't come. Instead the room grew even blacker. She realized she was losing consciousness and fought against it.

Sue flinched as bright beams of light swept across the room and over her. A blurred face appeared before her, and rough hands reached out to grab roughly at the lapels of her ruined uniform.

"Get it over with, asshole," she ground out through pain. She resisted as she was lifted, but the blackness returned and stole away the last of her defiance.

Confederacy Examiner Asler Kiis sat at the large oval conference table and listened with waning patience to the chaos around him. His long robes, although of the softest *chammiss* available, were heavy and irritating. The drone of constant chatter from the ongoing conference was also annoying, and the reason for calling the conference even more so. He tapped his fingers against the polished walnut surface of the table, admiring its quality and the striking pattern of the unique Earth product even as he planned his next move.

As Lead Examiner during the mission to contact the human race, he was also Examiner Advocate for the Earth people until such a time as the first Treaty between the Confederacy and the humans was complete. Whether the humans knew it or not, he was there to protect and defend them.

Of course, should the need arise he was also there to judge and punish as necessary. It was the highest position he'd achieved to date, and the most honor his clan had garnered in three generations. He was the youngest Examiner to achieve Advocate position in a hundred years, and he wasn't about to lose the chance to make history.

His entourage of fellow officers and Co-Examiner, Salis Fiiten, sat with him on one side of the table. All waited silently as the members of Earth's Starforce Marines argued among themselves on the other side. Or, at least some of them argued. Top Admiral Jeffers and Base Commander Davies sat as silently as the Confederacy team. These were the men to watch.

In many ways, Earth people were not dissimilar to his own, Asler thought, but most humans lacked the ability to touch each other as his people did, mind to mind. Perhaps this was why they were so loud and argued so much. Maybe if he had been older than his thirty years—maybe if he had been as aged as his predecessor—he could have continued to wait while the humans fought it out. But he wasn't.

"Enough." He echoed the thought aloud to Salis. Silently he mind-spoke to him. *"No more wasting time. Tell Admiral Jeffers we have made our decision, and if Earth wishes to begin Treaty talks with us, we must, and will, have control over this investigation into the attack."*

As he spoke the words into the mind of his partner, he stood, bringing the attention of the room back to him and his silent officers. In the first days of the initial Treaty talks a vicious attack had damaged both Inarrii and human starships. The Confederacy demanded a measure of control over the investigation into the attack, an investigation which the humans seemed determined to handle alone. The argument, not the first of its kind, had raged for the last half hour of Earth time, monopolized by the Earth military. It was not going to continue.

Salis, rising with his Co-Examiner, explained once again that the Confederacy would conduct the investigation or would break off the Treaty discussions.

Immediately several voices broke into heated argument. One caught Asler's attention—grizzled Earth Starforce Base Commander Davies, who until this moment had sat silently at the admiral's side.

"Captain Branscombe must be excused from any investigation!" the base commander demanded. His face was flushed and his words ripped through the clamor. "She's suffered enough at the hands of these terrorists," he insisted. "There is no reason to believe she had anything to do with this attack. She's been tortured, for Christ's sake."

"She may very well have been forced to give up the location of the base," interjected a young man. Asler had determined the speaker was a Starforce Lieutenant by his insignia and likely to be an Earth lawyer of some sort. The position was not one that Asler's race employed; with Examiners there could be no doubt when truth was determined, and therefore there was no need to argue over motivation, or punishment.

"Or perhaps she gave it up willingly after being with them this long," insisted another officer.

The argument had been heard before. What caught Asler's ear was the sincerity and concern ringing behind the base commander's words. The sentiments were echoed in his emotional projection. Obviously the old man cared for the woman as if she was his own child. The base commander's rage over her treatment and his fear over what might happen to her at the hands of the alien Confederacy tugged at Asler's heart. While Asler wouldn't enter another's mind uninvited, this man's emotions rose and pushed past the barriers of his mind and overflowed clearly into the room.

Asler's beliefs would never allow an innocent to be mistreated, but he had to make a demonstration of the Confederacy's power. The two compulsions pulled at him, and his head throbbed in reaction. There were factions on Earth that believed the Confederacy should leave, that for humans to work with aliens was an abomination. Their voices were a force, albeit a small one, in the human media.

As an Examiner, Asler knew his duty was to prove the Confederacy's strength by finding answers, and then to quickly mete out punishment where it was due. Perhaps the woman was innocent, but having been found on the vessel that had attacked the first scheduled Treaty talks, he too had to wonder how much she had told, how much she had been involved. As a Starforce Marine pilot she knew enough to be dangerous in enemy hands.

He squared his shoulders. Above all, the truth must be revealed. He signaled his entourage of fellow officers and as a group they stood beside him and Salis, and turned to leave the room.

"Wait," a voice filled with command called to them.

Asler turned back, already hearing the capitulation tinged with frustration in the mind of the Starforce admiral. Asler noted the power in his strong shoulders belying the heavy creases in his face. This was a man accustomed to the weight of responsibility.

"Admiral Jeffers," Asler responded, his trained voice perfectly even, uninflected with any emotion.

"The investigation is yours. You'll have full access to all our databases and scans of what happened. A complete record will be beamed to you immediately."

"And the surviving prisoners—the captured Starforce officer?"

The admiral's lips thinned. He laid a hand on the shoulder of the base commander who had protested so strongly, calming him with a gesture not unlike one Asler would use in the same situation. "They're yours." He raised his other hand as his grip on Base Commander Davies became stronger. "But you will consult us before any and all judgments are made."

Asler heard the iron in the admiral's voice, but he knew he had to be the stronger opponent in this confrontation. The Confederacy must have compliance. "You will not be involved in any judgment, Admiral. However, we will inform you before any punishments are meted out."

Asler turned and left as the protests began again behind him. His thoughts were grim as he walked quickly through the hallways of the Earth vessel toward his shuttle. It was doubtful this would be the last time the argument came up. Earth's people didn't trust the Confederacy yet—and how could they, really? They'd only been contacted a few months earlier. But if Earth was to be saved from pillaging by the larger universe, they must become part of the Confederacy. It was either that or be stripped of their resources by the pirates the Confederacy battled on a daily basis.

The more he interacted with Earth people like the admiral and the base commander, the more they seemed worth saving. But he needed data, needed to understand them better in order to fight for a decent Treaty for them. Despite being the Examiner Advocate for Earth, even despite the fact that his clan relied on him and his current rank to bring them status, he knew himself well enough that if he didn't believe in his cause, he wouldn't argue as effectively as he could. Earth had resources that the Confederacy wanted—metals and organics like the fine wooden conference table, and most of all imaginative, intelligent and culturally diverse people. In return, the Confederacy could offer protection and technological advancement for the planet. A Treaty would benefit everyone—Earth, the Confederacy, himself and even his clan, millions of light years away on their home planet Inarr. But he still wouldn't support the Treaty without having faith in the people.

He'd met only one human on a personal level at this point, not counting those attending the elaborate and lengthy Treaty negotiations. Earth's Starforce Major David Brown had made first contact with the Inarrii—or rather, they had contacted him. Major Brown was a strong and commanding presence, a man Asler enjoyed meeting. He spoke easily and commanded the men in his squad of fighter pilots with care and integrity. He handled his new role as emissary with equal care. Brown's personality had played a big part in the willingness of Confederacy representatives, like Asler, to begin Treaty negotiations with Earth that would greatly favor the humans, although they were likely unaware of the fact as yet.

"If we find their officer guilty, they'll never trust us," Salis stated flatly into Asler's mind. He paused in front of the entrance as the security scanner took his genetic imprint for comparison.

"They may not," Asler mentally replied. *"We'll know soon enough."*

Entering the softly lit shuttle, Asler felt immediate relief from the tension he'd suffered onboard the Earth vessel. There were too many unshielded people there, too many untempered emotions as people wondered about the Confederacy's arrival and what it meant to them.

Salis groaned and pulled his robe over his head, shedding the heavy garment quickly. Around them, other officers stripped as well, pulling off the clothing deemed correct for meeting this new species. Asler followed suit, stripping down to his *pettan,* a short-legged covering that wrapped him loosely from his waist to just above his knee. Earlier members of the Confederacy sent to observe human behavior noted that the Earth people wore many layers of clothing and suggested that wearing just the *pettan* in public might be considered disrespectful.

Inarrii were the perfect first contacts for Earth—they were shaped much like humans, though somewhat more muscular and about a hand's-breadth taller than a human's average height. Only their *L'inar* truly set them apart in appearance, the curving sienna-colored nerve lines that covered their skin from under their hairline, down the back of the neck and over most of their torso. There were many within the Confederacy who looked far more exotic. In some cases their appearance differed so much that humans might not accept them as friendly.

Asler lowered himself onto a low couch, letting the heat and vibrations from its cushions relax him further.

"Could I offer a calming moment, Examiner Kiis?" One of the female officers approached him. She reached her hand, palm forward to him, offering him as much comfort as he might desire in her arms. Physical touch kept the Inarrii calm and reduced the wear on their emotions caused by the psychic onslaught of close proximity to a species that did not shield their emotions. Sex was the common and often desired result.

Many of the younger officers were here for that reason, although the comfort would be shared by both participants. Behind her, Asler caught a glimpse of a grinning Salis shaking his head.

Asler stifled his own urge to smile. She was young and took her duties far too seriously.

"Thank you, but I'm about to review the investigation. The prisoner was badly injured, and I will need all my strength to deal with her. Perhaps Salis has some need to share with you."

She turned from him without any sign of rejection and made the suggestion to Salis. Now it was Asler who shook his head as his partner immediately took her up on her offer, a wicked grin spreading across his face as he led her away.

Asler's smile ended abruptly. He hadn't lied; he never would. Inarrii believed in truth, Examiners even more so. He knew the Starforce officer had been badly injured. She *would* need all his strength. He must discover what kind of threat the renegade forces that had attacked the first round of Treaty talks represented; he must know if the attack was based on irrational fear of the unknown, a common enough problem for first encounters, or if it was something more dangerous.

If the Treaty failed, so many of his efforts would be wasted. This one mission could make or break his future. While he had achieved much, his clan would still suffer as they had wagered a lot on his growing career. Anything that could stall or force the Treaty to fail must be stopped. If the human Officer Branscombe knew anything, he would have to discover it.